Caught in the Storm

By

Somisa Perpetual Hlangwana

Caught in the Storm

Caught in the Storm

Edited and Published by
William Jenkins
4036 Pine Street
Burnaby BC V5G 1Z5 Canada
williamhenryjenkins@gmail.com
http://williamjenkins.ca
Telephone: 1-604-685-4136

ISBN: Paperback 978-1-928164-39-5
ISBN: Electronic Book 978-1-928164-40-1
Copyright Somisa Perpetual Hlangwana © 2018

Caught in the Storm

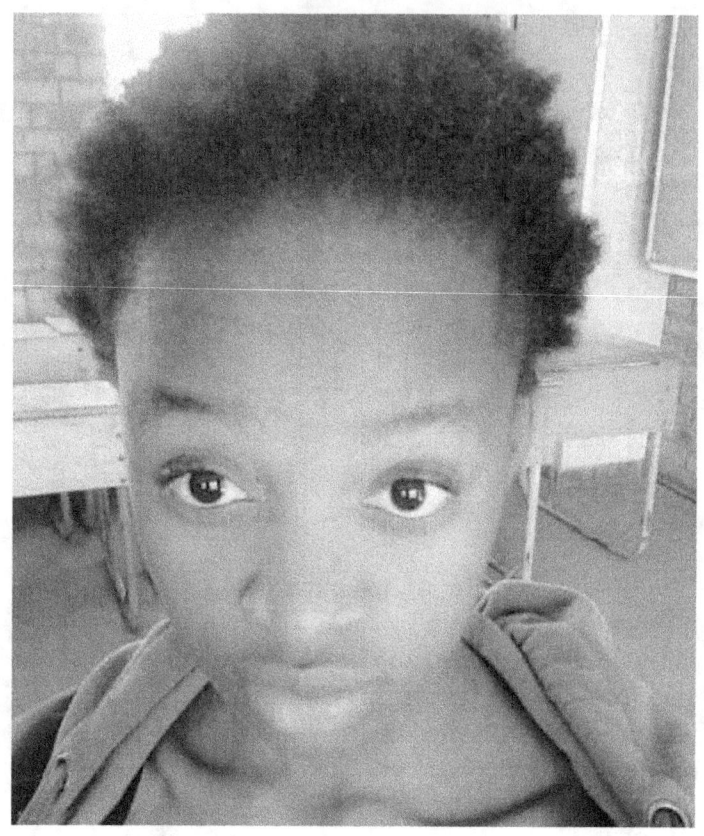

Somisa Perpetual Hlangwana

Biography

Somisa Perpetual Hlangwana was born in Thapane Village near Tzaneen in Limpopo Province in South Africa. Her birthday is May 30th 2001. She has three sisters but no brothers. She attended Thapane Primary School where she found she liked both reading and writing.

She won three reading competitions while in primary school. She loved literature and started noticing her writing talents when she was doing grade 9, when she wrote poems about herself. In grade 11, she fell in love with a short story titled "Transforming Moments", a story written by a famous South African writer, Qcina Mhlophe. Perpetual fell in love with the way the writer expressed herself and all the figures of speech. It made her jealous of Qcina's English and she wished she had been the author of that story. She thought of writing a novel and came up with "Caught in the Storm", her first book.

Somi felt that she could be a great writer only if she could base her writing on her own experience. She talked her Dad into getting her a tutor and then seduced the poor fellow just so she could know what true love is all about. Needless to say, Dad was not amused when he found that one of his daughters was pregnant.

Editor's note. Only after he agreed to publish this true life story of teenage life and love did Somi reveal that it was all in her imagination. She now claims virginal status, says that the tutor, although an ideal mate, does not exist. It's all "Fake News" to quote the current explanation for lies and deceit. This little liar is working on the sequel where I suppose she'll give birth to quintuplets each of whom will require a medical miracle to survive. I think Somi has a wicked sense of humour. If she's like this at 16, she'll probably be a politician by the time she reaches 21. In any case, if you want to know more about her, look for Somi Novelist on Facebook.

Somi thinks women deserve a special treatment and not only in ordinary relationships but also in marriage. Somi's story involves lot of worrisome things such as teenage pregnancy, the importance of education, how to take care of your loved ones, being disappointed or betrayed by those you love, true friendship, decisions in life, but mostly "love".

Somi dreams that some day she may change the world through her writing. She's writing not only for fun but also to motivate the youth on how to handle difficult situations.

To contact Somi by email, use

hlangwanaperpetual@gmail.com

or on Messenger:

Somi Novelist

Contents

Caught in the Storm

Chapter 1

Growing up can be fun, but it can be such a nightmare sometimes. Being separated from my loved ones was always my fear.

I grew up with my sister, Sthoko, who is two years older than I. I loved her and she loved me too.

When I was eighteen, I was staying with Dad and Mom only because Sthoko was doing her second varsity year and I was matriculating.

My dream was to find someone who would show me love, someone to embrace me in my difficulties, someone to show me the true meaning of love.

Some people dream of being rich, famous, etc., but not me. I, Somi Nkosi, always wanted to be married at a very young age. This always sounded crazy to my Dad, but he loved me anyway. And Mom? She understood because she had been married at the age of 20.

I was different because I loved school so much. I was doing grade 12. I was the best learner, but was not good at life sciences.

In the following weeks we were writing exams, but surprisingly we were given two weeks not to come to school but to prepare for exams. In our school it was like that.

I wanted to be a pharmacist, but how could I when I hated and wasn't good at life sciences? Dad was worried about this, but what was he going to do about it?

Caught in the Storm

Here's the story of my life...

I was born in Thapane village in Limpopo. At 18, I was in love with a boy by the name of Kgomotso. He was usually fine with me, but these days we seemed not to be hitting it off. I loved him so much, but I didn't know if he loved me back; he seemed to.

He and I would always fight, but that never changed the love I had for him.

We laughed together and we played together. He was the best comedian and made the relationship solid as a rock. He embraced me in my difficulties. He respected my choices and loved who I am. Regardless of anything, he adored me, it seemed.

He was doing grade 12, but in a different school. He asked to meet up with me. We met at our favourite spot, under the tree, sitting on a vast rock.

On this day, he was not in a good mood.

Me: Hey, honey, I hope I didn't keep you waiting.
Kgomotso: Hi.
Me: Oh and happy belated birthday. I'm sorry I couldn't be with you on your birthday last Saturday..
Kgomotso: You're sorry? Right on, people; she is sorry she kept me waiting. It was my birthday, but no, my girlfriend couldn't even spend it with me. Do you call this love?
Me: But you know I had to go to my Aunt's wedding. Please understand. I thought you weren't going to have a problem with it.

Caught in the Storm

Kgomotso: Somi, I'm getting tired of you and your family having tours. Your family keeps on taking you away from me. We never spend sufficient time with each other because of them. I think we should do the right thing.

Me: Okay; wait, what are you trying to say?

Kgomotso: Let's take a break.

Me: What? A break? Why, what break?

Kgomotso: Actually I'm giving you a break.

Me: I don't need a break. Kgomotso, please don't be like this. Are you just trying to break up with me?

Kgomotso: Look, I need to go.

Me: I asked you a question.

Kgomotso: You want me to answer you? Fine! YES, I'm breaking up with you. This is for us. You're not ready for the relationship so I'm setting you free.

Me: Really?

Kgomotso: Just giving you space. You surely need it.

Me: Are you sure of what you just said?

He left me standing with my mouth open wide. Why does it rain on me always? My boyfriend dumped me! He asked to meet me just to tell me it was over. He thought it was worth it? I loved no one but him. We had spent two whole years together. We had plans for the future. Yes, we are prudent. So, does it mean that it was all a lie? Did I have to let him go?

Chapter 2

I have a friend by the name of Thato. She and I became friends when we were still young, in the first grade. We became friends as my Mom and her Mom were close. My mother used to visit Thato's mother at their house with me. That's when I became close with Thato. She was cute, short, dark-skinned and innocent with angelic eyes. My mother likes her a lot and would always tell me that Thato was a good example for me. Thato wasn't really talkative, but she was understanding; a lot.

I always told her about everything in my life. On this day, I went to her house and found her watching TV alone and eating popcorn. When I got inside the house, I explained everything to Thato. I had to tell her everything as she was my best friend. That's how friendship works. No secrets should be kept and no lies; we both believed that. Then the friendship becomes as solid as a rock. Our friendship was not built on sinking sand, but on a rock.

Me: So what do you think, friend?
Thato: I think you should let him go. He surely is up to something.
Me: He called me, asked to meet me, tells me he wants to give me space because surely I deserve it. What's really going on? If I'm dreaming, then somebody should wake me up.
Thato: That's losing interest. Let him leave. That's for the best. These boys like hurting us; they think we can't live without them. Look, friend, let's just focus

on our books, we are Matriculating. I would never want to see you fail.

Me: Yeah, I hear you. Look let me go and take a nap, so as not to think a lot.

Thato: It's okay. Mom and I will be going to my uncle's place in about an hour, so I'll see you.

Me: It's okay. I'll go home. When are you coming back?

Thato: Tomorrow morning.

Me: Okay. Bye.

I thought about Thato's words all the way home. They were hurting, but full of truth. They healed my soul and helped my confused mind. She was my best friend and never consoled me with lies, but always was hurting me with the truth. It is better to be told the truth because the truth does set you free. Her words wiped away the confusion filling my head, but my heart was still refusing to admit the reality. This led me to call Kgomotso.

(He answered)

Kgomotso: What is it?

Me: Are you good?

Kgomotso: I am.

Me: Look, I miss you, Kgomotso. Can't you just give us another chance. Just one more chance.

Kgomotso: What chance? It's over. Is that too hard for you to understand?

Me: Kgomotso, really... Hello? Are you still there?

Did he just hang up?

This was hard.

Caught in the Storm

I was stressing like a barren,
a barren carrying a burden,
wanting a baby wholeheartedly.

I didn't want a baby,
I wanted joy.

My life was full of destruction,
my life needed instruction.

I wanted to do an investigation,
I didn't make an invitation.
I didn't invite this stress.
I wanted to know its formation.
I needed the whole information.

I wanted to install
my happiness through it all.
I wanted to be happy,
not crazy or even sappy.

My soul burned like an oven.
I felt as poor as an orphan.

When was I going to be glad?
Was I so sinful and sad?

Maybe the world is evil,
maybe this holds me still.

Is my life all done?
Right now it's not fun.

I need someone to make me smile,
but there's no one now for a while.

Was I guilty of something?
But I had done nothing.

Caught in the Storm

My life was getting exhausting.
My soul was now suffocating.

I was suffocating.

Yes, I was suffering because
everything under the sun is meaningless.

It's like chasing the wind...

I was the one who called and I was the one who was supposed to hang up, not him. He didn't want to talk to me.

Mom suddenly knocked on my bedroom door.

Mom: Knock, knock.
Me: Come in.
Mom: You look so bored.
Me: I am Mommy. Going somewhere?
Mom: I'm going to buy some veggies at the mall. Do you want to join me?
Me: Yeah, let's go, but you'll have to buy me pizza.
Mom: I knew it. It's okay, let's go.

We used Mom's car. Mom isn't working, but Dad just bought her a car as her birthday present. Lovely, right? They're such love-birds and Mom is my role model. We arrived at the mall and bought the vegetables.

Mom: Now we going to the bank to withdraw some money.
Me: I'm tired of walking. You'll come and find me at 'Debonairs'?

Caught in the Storm

Mom: Okay. Stay there; I'll come and find you when I'm done. Bye.

Mom left me and while I was busy walking at the mall, in front of me was a guy holding a bag and having another one on his back. I felt like helping.

Me: Hey.
The guy: Hi lady. Do I know you?
Me: No, you don't. I was thinking I could help you carry the other bag. It seems heavy.
The guy: Really? Well, I can't say "no" as an answer. I'm about to rest at that nearby shop. Where are you going?
Me: To buy pizza. Can't you just rest at Debonairs?
The guy: Yeah, that would be cool. No problem.
Me: So where are you coming from?
The guy: I was at the University of Johannesburg. I'm finally done with school now.
Me: Wow, that's nice. So where are you staying?
The guy: I stay at Fauna Park, in PLK city.

(His phone rang)
The guy: Sorry, Lady, I gotta take this call. Hello?... I'll be coming now. Okay cool. Thanks for letting me know.
Me: You have to go?
The guy: I really have to. Bye.

(He left)

Chapter 3

Mom then arrived and we went home. Mom and I couldn't even spend a second without talking. She was my best friend and she made me feel better. We arrived at 4 p.m. and I went straight to my bedroom. My sister called. She calls every day since she went to varsity. I suspect this was to make me feel jealous and want to be in varsity too.

Sthoko: Hey, girlfriend!
Me: Hi. Aren't you going to class today?
Sthoko: Umm, I'll actually think about that. I have a class in two hours. So, I'll decide if I'll go or not.
Me: Too good to be you. (I didn't mean it. I know Sthoko was only kidding. She wouldn't miss a class for anything.)
Me: And how's everything?
Sthoko: Everything is so wonderful. I'm enjoying being here.
Me: Oh, wow! Found a boyfriend?
Sthoko: No, not really, but there's this guy I'm in love with. It's a pity he just left as it was his last year.
Me: Oh, I hope you'll meet him someday. So you found him attractive?
Sthoko: Yeah . And how's everything there?
Me: Please don't ask... Kgomotso...
Sthoko: What did he do now?
Me: He left me, I couldn't see him on his birthday and he says Mom and Dad are taking me away from him. He's avoiding me he even blocked my number.
Sthoko: Did what? What's wrong with him?

Caught in the Storm

Me: How do I know? I'm so much worried, I can't even study.
Sthoko: No, just leave him and get back to your studies. You can't let him ruin your life. You can't lose yourself just because of a boy.
Me: Okay. Are you going to be here on my birthday?
Sthoko: No, I got a lot of work to do, but the day after your birthday, yes.

(Someone knocked)

Me: It's fine. There's someone knocking at the door.
Sthoko: It's cool. Send my greetings to Mom and Dad.
Me: Okay, bye.

I went to the door and opened it. There was a guy who looked very familiar.

Him: Oh hi. I hope I'm not lost. Is this Mr. Nkosi's house?
Me: Yeah. You're not lost. (Looking straight to his eyes and I tried to figure out if I knew him or not.)
Him: Okay, I'm Mangi. Is he around?
Me: Yes, he's in the shower. Wait don't I know you?
Him: Umm... I was with you at the mall this afternoon?

(Pointing at me with his finger)

Me: Oh yeah, I helped you carry a bag.
Him: Wow, it's you.

(I didn't know why he said "wow" but for sure it was for a good reason.)

Me: Yeah, come in. (With a smile.)

Caught in the Storm

He was handsome, looking good with white teeth shining bright. His voice was deep and I liked it. His accent was perfect. He had dimples. His body looked like that of a model. He was wearing a white short-sleeved shirt that traced his body. He was tall and light-skinned though he looked like a coloured.

He was the guy I was with at the mall and I was so much excited. I mean who wouldn't be, seeing such a knock-out again. So I sat with him in the sitting room.

Me: Want some juice or anything?
Mangi: Cold water, please.

His voice was deep and it warmed my bones.

Mom appeared from the bedroom to the kitchen and realised that Mangi had arrived.

Me: Mom, who's the guy?
Mom: He's Mangi, so says your dad.

(She left to go to the sitting room)

Me : Jeez, like I know who he is. (whispered)

I Went to the room and gave him water and sat down. Not so long afterwards Dad came.

Dad: Oh, here we are, Mr Kholoza. For how long have you been here?
Me: Just a second ago.
Dad: Okay. Thanks for coming.

I was swimming in sea of curiosity. What did he want? He thought I stole something from his backpack? That was the craziest thought ever. I just didn't know what to think.

Caught in the Storm

Dad: This is my wife and this is my daughter, Somi.
Mangi: Nice to meet you.

(We shook hands.)

He smiled at me. He knew me. I smiled back at him.

Dad: And he's Mangi. Hope he already introduced himself. Okay, Somi, as you've been given two weeks to prepare for exams, Mangi here is going to help you with Life Sciences until the day you're going to write.
Me: Oh, meaning?
Dad: He's going to be your tutor.

Chapter 4

My eyes opened wide. Dad and I hadn't talked about it before.

Mom: Only if it's okay with you.

(Silence)

Me: Yes, it is okay with me. When are we going start, Mangi?
Mangi: The day after tomorrow. Mr Nkosi, I'm sorry we won't be starting tomorrow. I'll just come back tonight at 8 p.m. to give her study guides and text books. I won't teach because I've just moved into a new house and there are some things I have to fix.

(He just moved into a new house? Gosh!)

Dad: It's okay, Mr Kholoza. Did your Dad give you the car, I mean the Audi you told me about?

("They seemed to be very close", I thought to myself.)

Mangi: Oh yes, he did.
Dad: Then you must be excited.
Mangi: Yeah a lot. So bye, family. I'll come back at 8 p.m. Bye Somi.
Mom: It's okay, my child, bye. Somi walk him to the gate.

Mangi was thinking "I don't know if there's something wrong with falling for the person you just met or not. I felt something inside whenever I looked at Somi. She just looked so fine to me and she made my heart melt. She was wearing trousers that traced her body. I didn't know if I should say she was dark-skinned or light-skinned; she was just looking fine. I swear this girl was her mother's photocopy; they looked alike. She had a very bright smile that made her face glow. Anyway, this girl is a princess. I wish I could grab her and run away with her, take her away from her parents. The fact that I am going to be her tutor... Wow!"

(As I was walking him out.)

Me: I thought you had forgotten my name already.
Mangi: How could I? I mean, it's just a simple name. I love your name.
Me: Hey, where did you meet my father?

(Folding my arms)

Mangi: At Letaba Hospital. I used to visit the hospital pharmacist just to know more about his work and I happened to meet your Dad. That's when he told me about you. He was using a different name for you, though. Petunia or something.

Me: Perpetual. That's my other name. He likes it a lot and you don't know how much I hate that name.
Mangi: It's cool, I'm going to call you that.
Me: I cannot believe you are going to annoy me every day, calling me that.

(We laughed together and he tapped my arm. His touch ran all over my body and I felt alive. So I seemed to be excited about this tutoring thing? Well, yes.)

Me: Okay, bye-bye then.

Caught in the Storm

(I lightly rubbed my nose)

Mangi: Bye, Somi.

Mangi left and Dad commented that this is the best thing he has ever done for me. My Dad believes in education and work. Mom believes in family and I believe in love. I needed love and sought it 'til I thought I'd found it, but you never know what the future holds, nobody does.

I went straight to my bedroom and was making a few calls to people I hadn't talked to in a while. Mom walked into my room.

Mom: I was busy doing the laundry yesterday and I didn't see your navy-blue jacket. Is it clean?
Me: Yes, Mom.

(I lied.)

Mom: Okay, give it to me so I can see it .

Me: Umm. Actually, Mom, I left it at Thato's place .
Mom: You know that the jacket is dear. Now go and get it.
Me: Mom can't I just get it tomorrow?
Mom: I said now.

(I could see that Mom meant it.)

My jacket wasn't at Thato's place. It was at Kgomotso's place . The other day when I was visiting with Kgomotso, we were tired and decided to take a nap. I forgot it.

I went out the gate and decided to go and get it. Maybe it was a good chance to spend some time with Kgomotso.

Before I get to Kgomotso's place, I pass next to this huge rock where Kgomotso and I used to chill. There were people sitting on it; a couple. They seemed to be having fun and reminded me of a lot of things and how my heart was broken.

I saw that the girl was wearing a navy-blue jacket looking like mine and the boy wearing grey trousers reminded me of everything. But hold on... who was I seeing? It was Kgomotso and this other girl, someone I didn't know. It couldn't be my jacket, no way. I went close and just stood there.

Kgomotso: Can we help you?
Me: Well, I was on my way to your place. I wanted my jacket.
Kgomotso: Oh...

(I quickly looked at the girl's jacket.)

Me: So you thought it was the best thing to do, to give her my jacket, Kgomotso! You thought it was worth it?
Kgomotso: Jeez, can't you just calm down. This jacket is not yours, but hers!

(Pointing at her.)

Kgomotso: It's funny you don't even know your own stuff.
Me : Oh?

Caught in the Storm

(I felt ashamed. Also, I felt like a fool in front of that short, chubby girl with short hair. Had I been too forward?)

Kgomotso: Anyway, this is Mbali. Mbali, this is Somi. She stays around.
Mbali: Oh, nice to know you, Somi.

(I ignored her)

Me: Can I have mine then.
Kgomotso: Go ask Mom to give it to you.
Me: But Kgomotso...
Kgomotso: Tell her I put it in her wardrobe.

(He interrupted.)

I left them.

Kgomotso had told Mbali i was just a girl staying around the village. So it was over between us. Tell me how sad that is. I went straight to his place and his Mom gave me the jacket. His Mom knew me. I went home crying. I hid my tears from everyone in the street. Have you ever cried and someone comes and talks to you in a happy manner without realizing you're crying? Then you just have to smile and talk back to them? Well, it happened to me this day. I smiled when people talked to me on the street. I smiled outside; inside I was crying and angry. Well, what doesn't kill you strengthens you.

Chapter 5

I went straight to my bedroom which was messy. I was too lazy to clean it. I wasn't really in the mood to do that. No teenage girl loves cleaning, I believed in that. On Saturday it would be my birthday. What birthday? Was it even going to be a birthday or a bad day?

I heard footsteps so I immediately wiped a stream of tears covering my cheeks. Mom knocked. She liked coming to my room and I disliked that. I let her in, though, as she was my mother.

Mom: Is the jacket.... Were you crying?
Me: No, why?
Mom: Your eyes are red. What's wrong?
Me: Mom, I wasn't crying. Oh yeah... my eyes are painful.
Mom: Oh shame, need to see a doctor?
Me: Huh? No, I'm now fine. I mean, I'll be fine.
Mom: Okay, why did I even come here? oh yes... your tutor will be coming here anytime from now, so I think you should be prepared.
Me: Oh?

(I had forgotten about him already. It was Kgomotso running in my mind always.)

Mom: And your Dad is taking me out for dinner tonight. We'll come back very late; don't wait for us.
Me: No problem, Mom.

(I don't know why I liked the idea. Don't get me wrong.)

Caught in the Storm

Mom and Dad left the house.

I was watching stories on my laptop and after ten minutes I heard a knock. I went to the door and opened it. I found that it was Mangi.

Me: Oh! Hey, come in.

He came in. I was excited and I didn't know why.

Mangi: You were sleeping?

Me: No i was watching a story, but we can go to the dining room.
Mangi: Yes, we need to get to know each other.
Me: Oh my gosh! Is it raining outside?
Mangi: Yeah, it is. I got a lift from my neighbour who is going fetch her girlfriend who stays around.
Me: Umm... should I give you a towel? Your shirt is wet.
Mangi: Are you serious, Somi? I'm fine. It's actually hot in here.

(He smiled at me and I blushed.)

He looked really good; his mustache was wet and it made him look sexier.

Mangi: Anyone around?

Me: Yes, two of them.

Mangi: Mom and Dad?
Me: No.
Mangi: Then, who are they?
Me: You and me.
Mangi: (laughs) You are so insane. Anyway, okay.
Me: Sorry (while laughing). Anyway are you good?

Mangi: I am doing so much fine. Are you ready for your final examination?

Me: Yes, I'm just not ready for Life Sciences.

Mangi: Don't you worry. I'll try to cover everything for you. Can I ask you something?

Me: Shoot.

Mangi: How old are you?

Me: I'm turning eighteen tomorrow.

Mangi: Oh, that's nice. I mean it's not bad at all.

Me: And you are?

Mangi: I just turned twenty last month.

Me: Hmm... and now you're expecting a job.

Mangi: Yes, I'm expecting a job.

Me: What did you study in Varsity?

Mangi: Umm... Pharmacy.

Me: Oh! I also want to become a pharmacist. I think you are too young to be expecting a job.

Mangi : (laughs) I know, hey. I started schooling at a very young age. And I know I look 18.

Me: (laughs) Actually, you look 16.

Mangi: No, don't I look 10?

Me: (laughs) That's too much now.

Mangi began to realize that nobody else makes him happy the way this girl does. He thought to himself "We laughed together. I'm falling for her. She is cool, charming and funny. After laughing with her, I looked straight into her eyes. I swear I really wanted to kiss her."

Mangi: Tell me, what do you like?

Caught in the Storm

Me: Me? Novels; poetry, writing; music and having fun.

Mangi: Oh wow! I also love novels.

Me: Something to do with Romance?

Mangi: Marriage.

(He raised his eyebrows.)

Me: And what's your favourite movie?

Mangi: Umm "Love at first sight".

Me: No no... that's my favourite!

Mangi: I guess we have a lot in common. Okay, I promised I'm just going to give you a few Life Sciences text books and study guides.

(He took them out of his back pack and held them to me.)

Mangi: Today's late that's why I'm saying we'll start the day after tomorrow.

Me: But, why not tomorrow?

Mangi: I'll be very busy.

Me: Oh, it's okay.

My phone rang It was Thato.

Me: Friend!

Thato: I'm missing you so much. I just got back from my aunt's place. Tell me, how's everything?

Me: What everything, I'm so hurt. He has a new girlfriend.

Thato: What! How! You guys just...

Me: I don't even wanna talk about it now. We'll talk, friend.

Thato: Yes we will.

Caught in the Storm

(She hangs up.)

Mangi: I know it's none of my concern, but is everything okay?
Me: Not at all, but I'll be okay.
Mangi: Oh?
Me: Yeah, I'm a big girl. I'm a tough cookie.
Mangi: Okay, let me get going. I'll come back the day after tomorrow for our lessons.
Me: Yes. Let me walk you out.

I walked him to the gate and opened it. Before he could get inside the car, he spoke.

Mangi: Bye, Somi.

I just waved.

Chapter 6

Mangi thought, "How was she a tough cookie? I did not care about that for I wanted to know what was going on. I just met her this day and I don't know why I cared about her this much."

I was caught in the storm without someone to make me feel better. I missed Thato. These days we rarely talked. Kgomotso was the only person who understood me. He made me feel better. He consoled me when I was stressed, picked me up when I was down. He made me smile when I was wearing a frown and took me as a friend. Where did all that go? Why did he press the pause button? He did it because he thought it was worth it? Who made him change his mind about me?

I might as well kill that person. If it's people, I might as well create genocide. I'll be locked in jail with my heart full of satisfaction if I do that, Because now I'm locked and bound with prison's chains and lamenting.

The same evening my phone rang.

Me: Hello?
Mangi: Hey, it's Mangi.
Me: Oh, hey. What a surprise! I didn't expect your call. Is everything okay?
(I then jumped to my bed)
Mangi: Look, I've been worried about you. What's really going on?
(He's really worried about me?)

Me: Do you have enough airtime?
Mangi: Yes.

(I told him about each and every single thing. I felt comfortable telling him about my private life, I never felt comfortable telling anyone about it besides Thato.)

Mangi: You surely don't deserve that, guy.
Me: Well, what can I say? I'll be okay.
Mangi: You will, hey. Any plans for tomorrow?
Me: I'm just gonna lie in bed. Think about it, on my birthday.
Mangi: Oh, that's boring. How about if we go out for movies tomorrow?
Me: I thought you were going to be busy.
Mangi: I can make time for us. Look, I mean, for you.
Me: Oh okay, I get it.

(Gosh, movies?)

Mangi: Yes, just to have fun. I hope you don't mind.
Me: It's - it's okay with me.

(I stuttered.)

Mangi: Then it's okay for both of us and I can't wait.
Me: You can't?

(I didn't know what to say)

Mangi: Yes.
Me: Oops, Mom is calling... bye.
Mangi: We'll talk tomorrow when I come to pick you up. Good night.

(He hung up.)

Caught in the Storm

Me: Mom?
Mom: I'm home. Open your door.

(Not her again.)

Me: You came home very late.

(I checked the time to see that it was 10 p.m.)

Mom: I know. And you were on the phone very late.

(Mom copied my thin voice. If only she knew how much I hated that.)

Me: Have you talked to Sthoko?

(I changed the subject so she couldn't ask who I was talking to.)

Mom: Yes. She's in love with someone, so she said, but they're not yet dating.
Me: She told me that too. The tintinnabulation, Mom, can you hear them?
Mom: Silly you, they aren't even dating yet.
Me: Finally she's in love, Mom.
Mom: Say that again, She never wanted a boy in her life. Before I forget, tomorrow...

(Scratching her arm.)

Me: Okay?
Mom: You and I have to visit your aunt for the whole day.

So I would have to cancel my plans with Mangi? No way. I had to say "No" this time. I've never gone out for movies with a boy. I do go to Cinemas with Dad and Mom, but it's boring!

Caught in the Storm

Me: Umm, Mom, I can't go with you.

(I didn't hear myself saying that.)

Mom: o. k. a .y... Why?

(Looking straight to my eyes with a curious eyebrow.)

Me: I've got plans.

(My tone changed.)

Mom: You got plans. What plans?

(She then sat at the corner of my big bed slowly.)

Me: I'm going out to the movies with ... with Mangi.
Mom: Oh, that's ...
Me: Mom, I know. I like him, Mommy. Please let me go.

(I interrupted.)

Mom: You'll have to ask your Dad.
Me: I'm afraid he'll say no. Mom, can't you tell him I went out with Thato?
Mom: You said you like Mangi?
Me: He's great. He wants to know my details. We have a lot in common. Mom, he gets me.
Mom: You can't be falling for a guy who you just met a few seconds ago.
Me: I know, Mom. He just wants to make my birthday a bit interesting. Don't tell me you have a problem with your last born having fun on her birthday.
Mom: Let me go get some rest. I have to drive tomorrow. Anyway, good night.
Me: Night, Mom.

Caught in the Storm

(When Mom ignores something it means she's not fine with it, sometimes.)

It was my first time telling Mom whom I like. Mom understood and that didn't happen often. Dad was going to kill me if I date Mangi. That I know.

I slept as it was late and woke up in the morning to do the house chores. Dad walked in the kitchen smiling.

Dad: Good morning, my baby. HAPPIEST BIRTHDAY!
Me: Dad. Thanks a lot. I'm glad you didn't forget it.

(We hugged.)

Dad: Come on. Has Sthoko called you?
Me: Yes, she said she was going to come back tomorrow. I can't wait to see her.
Dad: Yeah, also I.
Me: She's always been your favourite.
Dad: What do you mean?
Me: You like her.
Dad: Yes, she's my first born. I like you too. You're my last born.
Me: And my brother, Vuyo? You never talk about him.
Dad: He's married.
Me : You dislike him because he's not your biological son!

(I had a reason why I said that.)

Dad: Hey girl, where are you getting all of these things?
Me: Dad, if you love your three children equally, biological or not we'll see it as time goes on.

Chapter 7

So I didn't tell you about Vuyo. He's my big brother. My mother met Dad when she had Vuyo. My father didn't mind at all as he loved Mom. Vuyo's father broke up with my mother when Vuyo was one year old and Mom was 19. It broke my mother's heart knowing that Mr. Mtshali had another girlfriend and Mom had to leave him. Vuyo raised me up. He loved me; he grew up with me.

Knowing that we do not share the same father, Vuyo always wanted to know his biological father. He didn't care about the history between Mom and his father. My mother wasn't very pleased about that.

Vuyo, at the age of eighteen, in his first year of varsity, stayed with his Dad and step-mother. As I'm saying, Vuyo is now 24 and working as a doctor in Gemiston, where my mother comes from. Dad likes him, but not that much. Dad loves Sthoko. That makes me angry because Sthoko is my mother's and my father's child, but Vuyo was not my father's child. I missed Vuyo so much. Sometimes I wish he was still staying with us.

I decided to call him.

Vuyo: Happy birthday!

(He and his wife were on the phone.)

Me: Thank you, thank you, thank you.

(I chuckled)

Me: I miss you so much, guys. Like I'm in need of you.

Caught in the Storm

Vuyo: Aww, I'll come and see you. Guess what!
Me: You bought me a laptop!
Vuyo: No, silly you. My wife is pregnant!
Me: Oh no, you're lying!
Vuyo: I'm not. I haven't told Mom. I'll tell her today. She's one month pregnant.
Me: Congratulations, Siphokazi.

(That was her name. She was speaking Xhosa.)

Vuyo: She left to go to the bathroom.
Me: Oh, I'm so happy for you guys.
Vuyo: I am too. I'll make sure I come and see you on Monday.
Me: Okay, and Sthoko will be around.
Vuyo: It will be fun. I'll call you tomorrow. I love you so much, Somi.
Me: I love you more, brother.

Soon after my brother's call. I received a call from Mangi. Quickly I answered it.

Me: Hello?
Mangi: Hey, princess. Don't tell me you changed your mind.
Me: No. How could I?
Mangi: I'll be there in an hour. I'm still washing Nina.
Me: Oh, who's Nina?
Mangi: Pfft, she's my car.

(He chuckled.)

I couldn't wait to go out with Mangi. Going out with my crush; wait, did I just say my crush? Well, yes. I was now falling for him.

Then Thato called. My phone was hectic as it was my birthday. My Dad always says birthdays come once in year and they should be enjoyed. I liked the sound of that.

Me: Thato.
Thato: Happy birthday, friend!
Me: Oh, thanks.

(I smiled.)

Thato: Friend. You are sounding so... I don't know... happy?
Me: I know. Look I know. I'm so excited.
Thato: I was thinking of coming to your place just to chill with my friend. We haven't spent time in a while.
Me: Yes, so you want to come here and do what, because I'm going out for movies.
Thato: That sounds like fun. With?
Me: Smangaliso Kholoza.
Thato: The guy you told me about on WhatsApp?
Me: Exactly. I think he's into me or something. Or maybe he feels pity for me as I told him that my previous boyfriend broke my heart.

(I murmured the last part but Thato heard me it seemed.)

Thato: Whatever it is, you're about to find out. You sound ambivalent.
Me: I am. Let me just bath and get dressed. He'll be here anytime now.
Thato: Good luck and don't forget to use a protection.

The craziest friend I've ever had.

Caught in the Storm

I got dressed, looked stunning, glowing in my peach tight dress that traced my curves. I mean, I had a nice shape, if you didn't know that. I made a ponytail and my eyes looked even bigger, yet so cute. I was expecting something. Suddenly there was a knock.

Me: Coming!

(I opened the door.)

Me: Smangaliso.

(I smiled.)

Mangi: Wow! Greek Goddess.

(His tone was low that I couldn't even hear what he said.)

Me: Sorry?

Mangi: Let's get going before your Dad notices that I'm here.
Me: Cool.

We travelled, watched a movie. It was fun and romantic. He wished me a happy birthday.

Mangi: It was fun, wasn't it?

(We were now inside the car driving away from the cinema.)

Me: What was the name of the movie again?
Mangi: "You and me together, forever."
Me: Oh yeah. We should try it again, but no staring this time.

(What did I just say?)

Caught in the Storm

Mangi: Not seeing your face is hard. It's like catching lightning.

(I froze.)

Me: It's getting cold. We need to go.

(Changing the subject.)

We went to his place to fetch his jersey as it was getting cold .

Mangi: Umm, Somi. I'm thinking of... spending a night with you.
Me: What... no. My dad would kill me.
Mangi: He won't know. It's just to spend a night with you, nothing more. It's just to have a late night talk with you.
Me: Okay, yeah. I wasn't even thinking of anything. Let's talk.
Mangi: What was your dream when you were in primary?

Mangi thinking: I just love knowing about how people I love grew up. I find it adorable knowing about how they use to be when they were young and innocent.

Me: Seriously, now. I don't even remember, you know. I didn't have dreams.
Mangi: I wanted to be a chef.
Me: Oh. Can you cook?
Mangi: I think I'm the best.
Me: Wow your future wife will be very proud of you. I mean every woman wants a man who can cook.
Mangi: Yeah.

(He looked straight to my eyes.)

Caught in the Storm

Me: You're better than any other guys. You're just different.

Mangi: Talking of better, I made some cookies. I want you to taste them if you don't mind.

Me: No, bring them out.

He brought them. I tasted one and they were so nice.

Me: Wow! You can bake?

Mangi: I'm trying, girl.

After a while.

Mangi: Well, there's something on your upper lip.

Me: Oh?

(I was embarrassed. I tried to wipe it using my fingers.)

Is it gone?

Mangi: No, let me help you.

(He came closer to me. Our eyes locked and I felt millions of butterflies in my stomach. He held my chin up as he was taller than I and started kissing me.)

Mangi: Ahem.

(Pretending to clear something from his throat.)

Look, I'm sorry. I just... I didn't...

(He didn't know what to say.)

Me: It's okay.

Mangi: Okay, this is bad. I'm sorry, Somi.

Me: Uh, can you please take me home now.

Mangi: Of course. I mean sure. Where are my car keys?

He drove me home. The silence was noisy in the car. It was a weird silence until we had arrived to the gate when he broke it.

Mangi: Good night.
Me: Night.

He drove home. Thank goodness, no one was around. I was thinking about nothing but the kiss. So I decided to sleep. The scene repeated again as a dream. That's what happens to me. When I go to bed thinking about something, I'm going to have a dream about it.

I woke up very late the next morning. Dad came and woke me up.

Dad: It's nine and you're still sleeping. Your class will be starting in 30 minutes time.
Me: Morning to you too, Dad.

(I then yawned.)

Dad: Birthday fever?
Me: Huh? No. Let me take a bath. Where's Mom?
Dad: She went to work.
Me: But, she doesn't work.
Dad: She's just going to work for two weeks, replacing Ms. Khuse.
Me: Ms. Khuse, the receptionist?
Dad: Yes. Her husband just passed away so she can't come back to work anytime soon.
Me: Oh, that's sad. Aren't you going to work?
Dad: I'm waiting for your tutor to arrive.

Caught in the Storm

Me: Okay. Let me go take a shower.

Mangi arrived when I was done bathing. It was hard looking straight into his eyes. What did we do? Why did we kiss? I just don't understand why I kissed him when I knew it was going to freak Dad out.

Mangi: Sorry I kept you waiting, Mr. Nkosi.

(He was so embarrassed as though Dad knew what had happened last night.)

Dad: No, it's okay. You're just four minutes late. Look Mangi, things will be happening like this: My wife has found a job and I also work and you know that. Nobody will be around, just the two of you. So I don't need rubbish in my house. This is my daughter. No flirting nor dating. You're just going to help her with Life Sciences. Do you hear me, lad?

(He sounded serious.)

Mangi: Loud and clear, sir.

Dad: Good. I'm off to work. Bye, Princess.
Me: Bye, Dad.

My dad left. It was him and me now.

Mangi was thinking: Mr Nkosi is a very kind man and I like him for that, but he seems to be overprotective when it comes to Somi. If I am caught kissing her or even holding her hand, I know I will be dead. It is obvious he didn't want me to date his daughter; he said that simply because he didn't hire me for that. I love teaching Life Sciences a lot, but mostly I love Somi and I wish to have her in my life. She is adorable just like her mother. I'm going to keep on saying that she's her mother's photocopy because they look as though they were born from the same woman. They are both beautiful. Can't Mr Nkosi allow me to have what he also has? I have to stay away or I have to ignore the feelings I have for Somi. It is something I don't want to do, but have to do.

Mangi: Hi.
Me: Hey. You good?
Mangi: I'm fine.
Me: Look Mangi I'm sorry about everything that happened last night.
Mangi: No, it's okay. It's nobody's fault. Let's get started.

It was so weird of him, but I didn't worry about that. We went to my study room and he started teaching . I didn't pay attention, the kiss just couldn't just get off my mind. It was awesome and the best kiss I've ever had.

Mangi: Hello? Am I talking to myself?
Me: Huh, what did you say?
Mangi: I asked what GMO stands for.
Me: I'm sorry, Mangi I'm not quite up on this Genetics topic so I don't think I understood whatever you taught.
Mangi: Simply because you aren't paying attention. You are thinking about something else that has nothing to do with this lesson. What are you thinking about actually?

Caught in the Storm

Me: Mangi, you can't just act as though nothing happened last night. You kissed me and you enjoyed it. You kissed me! Me, Mangi!

(I was emphasizing the word "me".)

Do you remember it now?

(I was so annoyed.)

Mangi: Hey Ms. Nkosi. The kiss was a mistake. I'm your tutor and what happened last night will never happen again, so stop thinking about it.

(What mistake? He didn't feel it? He doesn't love me? Since when did he start calling me "Ms. Nkosi"?)

Me: Okay, it means I'm imagining things then.
Mangi: Yeah, bye.

(He was really acting weird.)

I didn't want him to leave. I loved him and didn't know what to do.

Well, he went home and at the evening, Sthoko arrived, happy, beautiful and looking nice. I was happy to see her. She was holding two big bags with clothes. She had put on a purple lipstick that made her look even prettier.

Sthoko: Happy belated, little sister!
Me: Thanks, sister.
Sthoko: I'm sorry I couldn't buy you a present, but next week I'll still be around. I'll make a plan.

(Her phone rings.)

She went to her bedroom. Dad and Mom arrived too.

Dad: How were the lessons?
Me: Great. He's good.
Dad: You seem to be down.
Me: I need to sleep.
Dad: But it's just 7 p.m.
Me: At what time do beds open, Dad?
Mom: Leave the baby.

I went to my bedroom.

Dad: She's not looking so good, Melisa. Anything you know that I don't know?
Mom: I don't know, honey. She'll be okay, maybe it's that time of the month.

Sthoko walked into the bedroom .

Sthoko: Why are you down? Kgomotso is cheating?

(Sitting at the corner of my bed.)

Me: We broke up and you know that. And now I fell in love with my tutor. My! I just love him.
Sthoko: Wow, you got a tutor. So this tutor guy, is he also interested in you?
Me: I think so. Yesterday he took me out. And we kissed. I want him to be mine.
Sthoko: Right on, sister! Be patient.
Me: I feel he's taking too long to tell me he loves me.
Sthoko: Patience is the key.
Me: So tell me, what's the name of your future husband?

Chapter 8

Sthoko: Well dear, Vusi. Every girls' man of their dream. Girls always were fighting over him even though he never wanted them back. He liked me, it seemed.

Me: That name is nice. He must be really handsome.

Sthoko: And classic too. He's fully mature with a well-built body. He wears shirts that show off his muscles.

(She was praising him and it reminded me of Mangi, he was like that too.)

Me: Hmm, wonderful. Can I have his numbers?

(I joked)

Sthoko: Hahaha, you're mad. I'm meeting him tomorrow. I can't wait.

Me: I'm happy for you. At last you're in love. And hey, Vuyo will be coming here tomorrow.

Sthoko Oh yeah .That's great news.

Me: Okay, let me make a call.

I went straight to the bathroom and called Mangi. I didn't want anyone to hear our conversation.

Mangi: Hey, Somi.

Me: Oh hi. I was expecting your call later on.

(Desperate me.)

Mangi: Oh I had a situation to deal with. What do you want?

Me: Mom and Dad are not around.

(I lied.)

Caught in the Storm

Mangi: Aren't you scared?

Me: No, my sister Sthoko just came back from University.

Mangi: Sthoko?

Me: Can you please come and fetch me. Look, I miss you.

Mangi: But it's late, I'll come and see you tomorrow.

Me: Okay. If you are just trying to save petrol, I could go there. I can use Mom's car.

Mangi: What? You can't even drive. Okay, I'll be there in about 30 minutes.

Me: Okay. Will be waiting.

(He hangs up.)

Me: Sthoko, I'm going somewhere; see you in the morning.

(I wore a gown on top of my night dress and went to the gate and stood there. After 25 minutes he arrived. I got inside the car and we drove to his house.)

Me: You hardly said a word inside the car.

Mangi: Somi, there's something I think you should know.

Me: You'll tell me tomorrow morning.

Mangi: Tomorrow morning? You're sleeping here?

Me: Mangi, am I annoying you or something? 'Cause since yesterday you've changed on me Smangaliso. You hate me right? Just be honest with me. Do you want me to go?

(He kept silent.)

Me: Let me just go, because you know what...

Caught in the Storm

(I walked to the door)

Mangi: Wait !

(I stopped and turned to look at him .)

Mangi : You said I hate you? Actually, I love you. I've been trying to deny this because I was afraid of your Dad. I respect him and if he finds out...
Me: Oh, you're serious?
Mangi: I am. If you feel that it's not a good idea for us to be together, I can give you time to think about it. I want to be with you.
Me: There's no reason to think about it. I love you more. I want to be with you.

(I said excitedly.)

I went closer to him and started kissing him whilst moving my hand over his body. I then took off his shirt. Slowly... slowly... boom! We made love.

After that I received a call from my sister.

Me: Hello?

(I was lying on his chest and he was playing with my long hair.)

Sthoko: Are you crazy? Mom and Dad will kill you.
Me: I'll come back early in the morning. I'll make sure they don't see me.
Sthoko: Actually where are you?

(I hung up.)

Mangi: You know all hell is going to break loose if you're father finds out about this.

Caught in the Storm

Me: He won't.

(Does the truth hide forever?)

I felt that I was the one who created the relationship. I was. I thought I should go for him before any girl would. I mean, everyone wanted to be with him because he was handsome, he had a car. Girls wanted him for that, but not me. I wanted him because I loved him. I wanted him because I thought he was the piece of my heart.

Don't fall in love because of what they have; fall in love with who they are because what you have can be taken away from you, but what you are cannot be taken away from you. That's just a fact that cannot be erased.

Me: What time is it?
Mangi: It's 4 a.m. Why?
Me: Take me home. I don't want to get you into trouble.
Mangi: Yeah, sure.
Me: Yeah, please now.

He drove me home and I called Sthoko to come open a gate for me. She came and we went to our bedroom and Mom and Dad didn't hear us.

Teenage life is hard. You want to do what pleases you and don't want to be controlled. I woke up very late in the morning and there was Sthoko in front of me looking so nice.

Sthoko: What do you think? stunning o' nah?
Me: Stunning, where are you going?

Caught in the Storm

Sthoko: I'm not going anywhere now. I'm just fitting because I'm having lunch today with Vusi, my boyfriend.

Me: Oh please, he's not one yet.

Sthoko: Whatever. Aren't you going to have breakfast?

Me: I don't want it.

Sthoko: When is your period date?

Me: I'm not sure. I think next week.

Sthoko: Exactly... That's why you don't want food.

She went to the dining room with her clothes changed. I called Thato.

Thato: Chomie (friend).

Me: Hey, any plans for the day?

Thato: Lying in bed the whole day. You!

Me: I was thinking of that. That's boring, as Mangi always says. How about if we go have a bite in a restaurant. Heard that there's a new restaurant in town.

Thato: I heard about it too, but where will you get the money?

Me: Vuyo is coming this morning. Surely he'll give me some.

Thato: Okay. See you then.

Me: 14:30.

Thato: 14:30 Is the time.

(We hung up.)

I went to the dining room.

Dad: Why aren't you eating?

Me: Pancakes aren't my favourite, Dad.

Caught in the Storm

There was a knock at the door. I went and opened it. There was my brother. I hugged him.

Me: You came alone?
Vuyo: Yes, I'll be here until tomorrow evening. Hey, family?
All of them: Hey!
Mom: You've grown, my baby, look at you.

(Mom's face full of joy and so glad to see her first born.)

Vuyo: Mom, please. Hey, Dad.
Dad: Hey son, you're even light-skinned now.
Sthoko: And you have beard now.

They all teased him and he was laughing his lungs out.

Vuyo: Everybody stop it. I haven't changed, okay?
Mom: And where's uMakoti (daughter-in-law)?
Vuyo: She's at home; she couldn't come. Mom, I don't know, but she's so moody this days. She doesn't want to eat anything else but her chocolate yogurt.
Mom: What?
Vuyo: Imagine, every day from work I have to come back with a yogurt or else she'll sleep in hunger.
Mom: (laughs) You'll get used to it, my baby.
Me: (laughs) I think you're having a good time in the house with your wife and everyone of course.
Vuyo: A lot, hey.
Me: Mind telling us what Siphokazi does beside the yogurt saga?
Dad: You're so naughty, Somi.

Caught in the Storm

Sthoko: Come on, Dad, let Vuyo proceed.
Vuyo: Well one of the days... guys, please, this is crazy, okay. Now Somi pass me the pancakes.

It was nice having him around. It made me feel just fine and so much fun to have a big brother. My eyes were always gleaming with tears during his presence. What tears? Tears of happiness and gratitude.

Mom: So, ever thought about the name you're going to give to the child.
Vuyo: Well Mom, what I can say is that I'm expecting a baby boy and i want his name to be...

(He looked at Dad)

Vuyo: I want his name to be Nathaniel.

(Silence.)

Nathaniel was his father. We could see Vuyo loved him so much. He might not have raised him but he loved him.

Mom: Why Nathaniel?

(She look at Vuyo with a curious look after sipping her coffee.)

Me: I like it. It's a nice name.

(That was me, always standing by my big brother.)

Dad stood up and exited. Surely he didn't like the idea as Nathaniel Mtshali. Vuyo's father had left him at a very young age but still Vuyo took him as the better father. I didn't blame Vuyo sometimes; a father is a father regardless of anything.

Caught in the Storm

Sthoko: Oops
Vuyo: Mom, I love my father.
Sthoko: But Dad is not Nathaniel.

(Sthoko liked making things hard)

Vuyo: My real Dad is Nathaniel.
Me: I didn't know. Well Mom, I don't see a problem with Mangi giving the child his father's name. I mean Mom, even Vuyo was your Dad's name too.
Sthoko: Too weird. I gotta go and prepare myself, I'll be going out soon.

(She exited.)

Mom: It's still fine, Vuyo.
Vuyo: Thanks, Mom. And Somi, I bought you these for your birthday.

He put a brand new laptop and a diary for the next year on the table.

Me: Oh thank you, thank you so much. You know me very well.

I hugged him. I was so excited. I took it to my bedroom and he followed me.

Vuyo: I'm glad you like it .
Me: I do a lot! I'm asking money to go to a new restaurant in town with my friend.
Vuyo: Okay.

(He took out R700.)

Me: Ah that's a lot. Thanks, brother.
Vuyo: Is Thato still your friend?

Caught in the Storm

Me: Yes, we'll be going at 14:30. I'm sure you have missed Calvin. You probably can go with me when I go to Thato's place, so to see your friend.
Vuyo : That's what I'm thinking about .

Calvin was Thato's brother who was doing his last year of varsity. He was doing Chemical Engineering in Witwatersrand University. He was my brother's best friend since they were young.

It was now 14:00 and Sthoko had gone to her date.

My brother and I went to Thato's place. Thato and I went to town and I was telling her about everything that has happened.

Thato: Oh I hear you. You were obviously going crazy, but... did you guys use a protection?
Me: Umm. No, we didn't.
Thato: What if you become pregnant?
Me: How can you think of such things?

We walked into the restaurant and i was shocked by what I was seeing. Sthoko was with the guy she had told me about. They were kissing... Vusi....Vusi was Mangi, my tutor.

Chapter 9

Thato: Is that what I think?

I couldn't say a word. My big eyes were now opened wide. I rubbed my eyes just to ensure if it was a dream or not, it wasn't. I couldn't say a word.

We went closer to them and Thato was following me with worry on her face. She never wanted to see me hurt.

Me: We just started dating last night and now you're here kissing my sister, having a good time! You were fooling me?

(People's eyes in the restaurant were looking at us; I didn't care.)

Mangi: Baby, look, this is not what you think.

(I could see a worry on his eyes and a confusion on my sister's.)

Sthoko: Okay, what's going on, lana?
Me: That's my boyfriend... you know what, Mangi...
Thato, let's leave this place.
Mangi: No baby, wait!

He ran after me.

Mangi: Can I just explain.

(I raised a curious eyebrow.)

Mangi: I didn't know she was your sister.

Me: Still that doesn't make things better. Look, go back to her. Leave me alone. I never want to see you again.

Mangi: And our lessons?

Oh, so that's all he's worried about?

Me: Look, I don't care. I'll tell Dad to look for somebody else, because you, Mangi, you're a snake that bites people and leaves them, simply for sheer fun of biting them.

Mangi: Baby! Please don't say that.

Me: Goodbye, Mangi. It was good knowing a person like you. Friend, let's go.

We left him standing there.

Mangi thought to himself: I messed up. The only reason why I asked her about the lessons is not because I was worrying about money. No, I wanted to be close to her. I cannot afford to lose a Greek Goddess, no way! I'm not going to give up on her. If I have to do anything just to win her back, I will do that.

He then returned to the restaurant, his hands on his head. People were staring at the guy who had just messed up. He felt really badly.

Sthoko: That was, I don't know, bad?

(sarcastically)

Mangi: Yes, which is the reason why I have to leave right now.

(He then paid for the bill)

Caught in the Storm

Sthoko: Why do you have to leave. You didn't finish your food.

Mangi: I don't care about the food. I care about your little sister. Now goodbye, Sthoko.

Sthoko: And me?

Mangi: You? Sthoko this thing is crazy; there's no future between us.

Sthoko: So there's a future between you and Somi?

Mangi: Maybe yes, maybe no.

(He then left.)

Thato: You think it's a good idea what you did?

Me: Do you think it's a good idea what he did? I loved him. What have I done to these boys?

Thato: Are you sure you need a new tutor?

Me: No, he's the one I understand. I don't know what I'm gonna tell Dad. I don't want to put him into trouble.

Thato: Exactly.

Me: What am I gonna to do now?

Thato: Umm... Let him be your tutor, just your tutor.

Me: Just like that?

(Silence.)

Me: I think that's best.

Thato: You see?

Me: We've arrived. Look, let me go.

(We hugged.)

I went home. Mom, Dad and Vuyo were in the dining room.

Mom: Look who's back. Come join us.

Caught in the Storm

Me: I have a headache; I need to sleep.

Mom was persuaded by the way I acted, but they knew something was wrong as I've been acting weird in the past few days.

They were surprised. I walked straight to my bedroom and made a call. I called Mangi.

Mangi: Thank goodness. I've been trying to call you and your phone...
Me: Would you just shut up and listen to what I want to say?
Mangi: I'm sorry.

(With an apologetic voice.)

Me: Yeah, you should be sorry. I'm the one who called. You can still be my tutor.

Mangi: Oh thank you, you know.
Me: But just to be my tutor.
Mangi: This means a lot, Somi.
Me: Okay, yeah, bye.

Mangi felt he had never been so miserable in his whole life. He was so lonely and his big house was so quiet. He was thinking "What was I expecting? I'm staying alone. I just wish Somi were here; I miss her. Today's been the worst day of my life. I lost a biggest part of me, a girl so innocent with the longest hair. I lost someone who wanted to risk their life, by driving at night, just to come and see me. I'm not going to forgive myself. I love the girl."

Caught in the Storm

Sthoko came back home and opened my door. My heart was in my throat.

Sthoko: So your tutor, it's Vusi?
Me: Actually my tutor Is Mangi.
Sthoko: I don't see a reason for your anger. We both didn't know. We fell for the same guy; we both didn't know!
Me :He told you he was Vusi?
Sthoko: And Mangi also, but I preferred Vusi.
Me: Are you guys dating?
Sthoko: No. Look, I'm sorry. You can have your man.
Me: It's over between the two of us.

My voice was so low, as It was affected by the worry I had. Mom walked into my room.

Mom: What's this noise all about?
Me: Mom, the guy Sthoko have been telling you guys about is Smangaliso.
Mom: Oh no?
Sthoko: Look Mom, I don't wanna ruin people's relationship. Let them continue.
Me: Mangi and I are dating, Mom. We actually broke up so things can go back to normal.
Mom: Can we talk tomorrow?
Sthoko: Yeah sure, Mom. Today was too long, let me head to the bathroom.

My phone immediately rang. It was a private number.

Me: Private number, hello?
P.N: Hey, I wanted to wish you a good night.

(The person sighed and the voice sounded familiar.)

Caught in the Storm

Me: Thanks and good night to you, too, but who are you?

(I knew it was 'him'.)

P.N: It's Mangi.

I hung up.

This time I missed Kgomotso. He loved me, he would make me smile. I remember the other day he wanted to see me, but couldn't as I wasn't allowed to go out. Kgomotso came to ask for water to drink to my place just to see me. That was love.

(Tears were in my eyes.)

Where did that all go? Why is life full of changes and surprises?

We all went to the dining room and my brother was preparing to go.

Me: I can't believe you're leaving. I'm going to miss you.
Vuyo: Don't worry I'll still come back again.
Me: I love you, Vuyo.
Vuyo: I love you more, Somi. Come here.

(I hugged him for a long time.)

Vuyo: Are you okay, Princess?

(He whispered in my ear.)

Me: I'm fine, brother.

(I whispered back.)

Vuyo: Bye, everyone.

Caught in the Storm

Vuyo went home. Dad and Mom went to work. Mangi came after 30 minutes.

Me: You came earlier than expected
Mangi: I know. Are you okay? (I could see the embarrassment on his angelic eyes.)
Me: No, my eyes are sore. My mother says it's because I'm always on my phone.
Mangi: You think it's true?
Me: Of course. Yes. What were you expecting.

(I folded my arms with a rude attitude.)

Mangi: Jeez, no need to be harsh. And I'm still sorry about yesterday.

Sthoko came to the kitchen.

Sthoko: Hi, Mangi
Mangi: Hey.

(She switched off the stove)

Me: Going somewhere?
Sthoko: Taking a walk.

(My sister was worried, true. Did she love Mangi that much?)

She walked out

Me: Hmm. Okay Mangi, let's go to the study room.
Mangi: Okay. Today we're going to learn about 'Reproduction'.

He went on and taught. He taught me the whole Chapter. Then we were taking 30 minutes of break and we didn't know what to do. Things were just

Caught in the Storm

awkward. There was silence and I took my phone out and decided to chat with Thato. I was receiving a lot of notification alerts from WhatsApp as I haven't been using it for a long time. I pretended to be smiling and laughing at messages which weren't even funny just to make Mangi jealous. He got irritated and took out his phone too. He put his phone on vibration because whenever he received messages the phone would just vibrate. I guess that was to avoid the noise as mine was irritating.

Mangi: Okay that's enough, Somi! Put the phone down.
Me: Who's phone?
Mangi: Yours obviously.
Me: okay mine! We are not learning right now, are we? And regardless of that I'm not your girlfriend, am I?
Mangi: Okay fine. I'm sorry then. I was just...
Me: Weird, of course.

Mangi thought "Weird"? I was not weird, I was just jealous. How was she blind to realize it. Wasn't it obvious? The more she was giving me the dirty attitude, it made me adore her more. She would pout at the end of each sentence. This girl was so pretty and I don't want to lose her.

Mangi: Let me go have something to eat at the mall. I'll come back after 20 minutes.
Me: Fine, Mangi.

Well, I didn't mean what I said. I missed Mangi. I know if we were fine and not having the tension we were having, we would be flirting and smiling at each other. But hey... I waited for him and I couldn't wait to see his face again. I'm obsessed with the guy.

Mangi: Sengi buyile (I'm back) I'm from the shop. I bought us pies.
Me : Thanks. Let's get to the next topic then we'll eat them. Before that, let's become friends again, Mangi.

What did I just say?

Mangi: You're sure, Somi?
Me: Yes, why not?
Smanga: Okay. Good idea.

Mangi thought it wasn't really a good idea. He didn't want to be her friend and she didn't want that either. He knew because he knew she loves him. He thought "Well, if being a friend means her being part of my life, that's okay. This friendship thing isn't going to work."

Somi realized that he has taught me for two hours and it is now 4 o'clock and Sthoko still isn't back yet.

Mangi: I'll give you a task to do concerning what we were doing. You'll submit it, the day after tomorrow.
Me: No problem.
Mangi: Somi, have you forgiven me?

(He held my hand.)

Me: Yeah. I do forgive you.
Mangi: I'm grateful.

Chapter 10

After a month, we had started with our exams and they were not so hard. We were going to finish with Life Sciences and Mangi and I had enough time to keep the syllabus going. We were now becoming friends. Even though I still had feelings for him, I couldn't tell him due to my ego.

Thato came to my place so we could study Geography or should I say 'review' Geography? We were always talking about Mangi. We wouldn't talk about her boyfriend as she was single since the previous three months. She said she was tired of getting hurt. She believed that relationships weren't real. She just stayed away from love.

Thato: Wonderful!
Me: My friend, I've been feeling strange and now I'm feeling dizzy you know.

(Pause)

Me: What are you thinking about now?
Thato: When last was your period?
Me: Last month, I think.
Thato: Oh, check your period calendar.

I checked my period calendar on my phone and I was eight days late.

Me: I'm just eight days late, not bad.

Thato gave me a certain look.

Me: What?
Thato: Aren't you pregnant?

Me: What! No. You think so... I can't be... Am I?

Thato: I don't know, Somi. What if you are?

Me: I never was this late before, but it does happen. Hey, I'm not pregnant.

Thato: We should get a pregnancy test.

Me: You're stressing me now.

Thato: I'll go get it tomorrow. Mom and I will be going to town.

Me: Okay. You'll hit my hotline when you're back? If I'm pregnant, my parents would be ashamed, disappointed, hurt. And my brother, Vuyo? I don't think he'll be pleased. People at school? I'll be a laughing stock. If I'm pregnant, it'll mean no varsity for me next year. What is going to happen now; what about my dreams?

Thato: Don't be stressed, okay. You know that kills me. Let me just get going. I'll see you tomorrow.

Me: Please don't forget.

Thato: I won't, I promise.

Thato went out of the house. I kept watching my stomach to see if it was big or not. Well, there were no signs. Of course there wouldn't be. Even if I am really pregnant, it is too early for that.

Sthoko: Are you okay, little sister?

Me: Yeah, I just need to write a task, then we shall talk.

Sthoko: Alright.

Sthoko went to the sitting room and I started writing my tasks and stuff. Thato called me.

Me: We'll talk later. Right now I'm busy.

Caught in the Storm

Thato: I found a pregnancy test in my mother's drawer.

Me: Oh really? Meaning I should come now?

Thato: No. You'll come tomorrow morning or evening. I'm sure you're not pregnant; do not stress.

Me: I'm so scared.

Thato: Don't be, my love. Whatever it is, we're about to find out.

Me: Yeah.

Thato: Good night.

Sthoko came inside my room as she was out when I was on my phone.

Sthoko: Scared of what?

Me: That's eavesdropping.

Sthoko: I call it caring about you.

Me: You were listening to my conversation?

Sthoko: Are you hiding something?

Me: What? No.

Sthoko: Come on, Somi; you can tell me everything.

Me: You don't really care. You're just curious, Sthoko!

Sthoko: The truth does come out.

Me: Okay, I'll tell you. I think I'm pregnant.

Sthoko: What! Didn't you use a protection?

Me: No.

Sthoko: Somi, why?

Me: It was my first time and I forgot to remind him about it.

Sthoko: Mangi, right?

Me: Yeah, Mangi.

Sthoko: I'm wordless.

Me: I need to sleep.

Caught in the Storm

Sthoko: No matter what, I'll always be beside you.

"If I'm pregnant", I thought again, "things are going to be difficult. Mom and Dad are going to kill me and burn my body into ashes. If I'm pregnant then it won't be fair at all. But wait... Is life fair overall? I'm a baby as Mom calls me and I couldn't afford to have a baby. I don't even know how to feed a child. I'm even scared of holding a newborn baby; they're so soft and tiny. What if Mangi abandons me and runs away? Why didn't he use a protection? Because he wanted to give me a child and ruin my future? No way! No! I want to know right now. I want to know if I'm pregnant. I want to know what will happen when everyone finds out that I'm pregnant."

I slept and woke up in the morning at 5 a.m. It was cold outside. I then bathed and went to Thato's place. I knocked on her window. She came out.

Thato: You came very early. Let's go inside.
Me: Where's your Mom?
Thato: She's still sleeping. Come in.

She handed me the pregnancy test kit.

Thato: Go to the bathroom and then come back and tell me the result. Good luck! I went to the bathroom and came back after some few minutes.

Thato: What did you result in?

Chapter 11

Me: I'm pregnant.

I shed a tear that ran fast out of my eye. I didn't know if I should scream or go hang myself. I thought of Mangi and I hated him for impregnating such a wonderful soul. I didn't deserve to be pregnant at my age. I'm too wise for that. Thato couldn't say a word. She was worried as though she was the one who was pregnant. She felt for me. She was wordless, I could see that.

I cried so hard as I didn't have a choice.

Thato: Friend, please. You're making me cry now.

We both cried. It seemed insane, but that was a true kind of friendship. That's the kind of relationship we all need. A friend who cries with us, laughs with us, is always by our side, a friend who knows what's really in our hearts and what we need. I call that a true bond.

Me: Can i be with you the whole day?
Thato: I don't think that's a good idea.
Me: Why? Because you don't understand?
Thato: You have a class at 8 and will we tell your father?
Me: Do I look like I'm interested in learning, Thato? I'm not in the mood for learning.
Thato: You don't want to fail life sciences. Do you?
Me: You're right. I'm lazy to go home. I'll stay here till 8. Mangi will fetch me
Thato: Yeah, it'll still be fine .

Caught in the Storm

(Silence.)

Thato: What are you thinking about?
Me : You think I should tell Mangi about the pregnancy?

(I was lying on Thato's lap, my hair messed up like the grass in the wilderness)

Thato: Of course. It's his baby, isn't it?
Me: No, it's too early. You know I still love him. And the fact that I'm going to have a baby with him... I think we should fix things.
Thato: Did you forgive him?
Me: I did, but I told him I couldn't be with him again.
Thato: You meant it?
Me: Not really. What if he runs away after hearing that I'm pregnant?

(My phone rang.)

Me: Speak of the Devi... hey, Mangi.
Mangi: I'll be coming in 30 minutes.
Me: Could you please fetch me at Thato's place?
Mangi: Okay, no problem.
Me: Wait, before you hang up. Have you cooked?
Mangi: No, why?
Me: I wanted you to come with something to eat, but anyway it's okay.
Mangi: I have fries and a soft drink. Should I bring you them?
Me: Oh yeah. Can you please hang up, Dad's calling.

(He hung up)

Caught in the Storm

Ugh Dad

Me: Hello.
Dad: You aren't in the house. Where are you?

(There we go with the "overprotective Dad", Can't he notice that I'll be a mother soon?)

Me: I'm at Thato's place.
Dad: So early?
Me: Yeah. Anyway, it's my last day of learning.
Dad: Okay. I just wanted to know where you were. Bye.
Me: Friend, I don't even know how I'm going to face him.

After a while, Mangi arrived. We were standing at the gate.

Mangi: Hi, Thato.
Thato: Hey, Mangi.
Mangi: "Sowmi".

(That was just the way he pronounced it, so sweet.)
Me: Mangi... Chomie (friend) I'll see you tomorrow.
Thato: I'll make sure I call tonight.
Me: Okay, bye.

(We hugged and she whispered "Everything's going to be alright", in my ear.)

Mangi drove.

Mangi: You guys are friends indeed.
Me: And in need.

Mangi looked at me.

Caught in the Storm

Me: What is It?

He stopped the car, came closer to me and started kissing me inside the car. We kissed for one minute. Then he started driving. I was blushing when he looked and smiled at me.

Me: What's going on between us?
Mangi: I don't know. What I know is that I love you and you love me too.
Me: Obviously.
Mangi: Can't we just make up this thing of ours. I need you back.
Me: Honestly, Mangi, I also want you back.
Mangi: Wow, meaning we're cool?
Me: Yes, Mangi. I've been missing us and I couldn't tell you because I was...
Mangi: Egotistic.

(He finished my sentence then chuckled.)

Me: No silly, because you were a **jerk**.

(Emphasizing the word "jerk")

Mangi: I know. Look baby, I'm sorry, hey.

Me: It's okay. Now drive a little bit faster. Time is money.
Mangi: Okay, Ma'am.

(He chuckled.)

If only he knew that I was carrying something that was going to destroy his mood. If only he knew he was going to be a father in few months' time. Then he wouldn't be happy. How am I going to tell him? Break his heart? I love him and don't want to break his heart. While he was driving and smiling, it dug a hole in my heart because I was going to spoil his mood by telling him the "bad" news.

Mangi: Hello? What are you thinking about?
Me: No, I'm just, you know, thinking about us. I truly missed you.

(He kissed my forehead.)

We arrived and as usual he did his work and it was his last day and everything was covered.

Mangi: Did you write those tasks?
Me: They're in my bag. They were so easy. Today you seem excited.
Mangi: Yes. You made my day

(Is telling you that I'm pregnant going to make your day Mr Kholoza", I wondered.)

Me: Wow, Okay.

Sthoko came into the study room.

Me: Umm, Sis, is everything okay?
Sthoko: I was just wondering if you need coffee...
Me: Not really.
Sthoko: Sorry for interrupting cute conversations.
Me: You mean lessons. Look, close the door behind you.
Mangi: She's weird.
Me: Is she?
Mangi: Yeah. I just wish I could just get a job. My qualifications are perfect.

Caught in the Storm

(I knew he just wanted to change the topic, but anyway, it was for the best.)

Me: That's better. I wish I was done with school.

(I groaned.)

Mangi: Don't worry, next year is your varsity year; you're almost there.

(I kept quiet and looked down.)

Mangi: Baby, did I say something wrong?
Me: No, actually next year... Look, I need a gap year.
Mangi: That's mad. Why?
Me: Because I'm pregnant!
Mangi: Huh?
Me: I'm pregnant with your child, Mangi.

(Tears started flowing.)

Mangi: You're pregnant? Wow... Meaning I'm going to be a father!?
Me: Yes, Mangi.
Mangi: I'm so excited and confused at the same time.
Me: Why excited?
Mangi: Simply because I'm going to have a baby with you.
Me: What? Why confused?
Mangi: I never noticed I didn't use a condom. Baby, I don't know what to say. I'm glad, for how long?
Me: I think this is thirty days pregnant.
Mangi: Oh, wow!
Me: How can you be excited now?
Mangi: Come on, Somi. The person I love is pregnant with my child. What were you expecting?

Caught in the Storm

Me: You think we should tell Dad?

Mangi: We should tell him when he comes back.

Me: What? As easy as you say it? You know he's going to kill me. Actually both you and me.

Mangi: Then he'll have to go to hell. You're not ten, you're actually eighteen.

Me: That doesn't make me a woman, I'm still their baby.

Mangi: You meant their child? You're not a baby.
Your parents must let you grow .

Me: Mangi, stop it.

Mangi: I'm sorry. Actually I don't think your Dad will have a problem with him having a grandchild. He'll probably be happy for you.

(Does this guy even know the man we talking about?)

Me: Maybe you're right, hey.

(I was just ironic and consoling my broken heart.)

Mangi: But, I'm scared, Somi.

(What's wrong with this guy with mixed emotions.)

Me: I am too.

Mangi: Your Dad is going to chew me alive.

Me: Please don't even mention that.

It was verified I was pregnant. It was confirmed my life had now changed. I had to tell Dad and that killed me. The truth always comes out and I hate the sound of that. I could see the fear or terror that covered Mangi's face. All you could see me do was cry, tears falling like waterfalls. My heart was beating fast and louder than a drum. Where was I going to hide?

Chapter 12

Again, it was just all a lie. Dad was going to be happy knowing that his child won't be going to varsity the next year? That sounded crazy.

Well nobody knows what the future holds. You get to know when the time comes. Mom arrived after some few minutes. She came straight to the study room. Blood was running through my veins. I was terrified.

Mom: Chatting in the study room, huh?
Me: Because we're done with everything. Where's Dad?
Mom: He said he was going to buy Sthoko pizza.
Me: Oh nice.

(And me? I thought to myself.)

Mom: Oh and how are you guys, everything fine, Mangi?

(He looked at me.)

Me: Mom knows about us.
Mangi: Ohh... We're actually fine and thanks for asking.
Mom: Oh, that's pleasing. So you're done with the work?
Mangi: Yeah I-I am.

(He was stuttering.)

Mom: And did he pay you?
Mangi: Yeah he did and I'm satisfied.
Mom: That's wonderful. Here they are. You guys came back very early.

Caught in the Storm

Dad: Oh yes. There weren't many people today, fortunately.

Sthoko: And Dad was so happy as he was complaining all the way about us going to wait for ages.

Dad: Hey, I'm old now and I hate to stand for too long.

They all laughed besides Mangi and me.

Me: Dad, can we go to the sitting room so to talk about something really important.

Dad: Oh, okay. Let's go inside.

My! Dad looked happy. I was going to spoil his day; that I knew. We went inside, my heart in my hands. I was scared, terrified. What was going to happen when I tell Dad I'm pregnant?

I can imagine the shame in my Mom's eyes. Vuyo was going to be disappointed. Mangi looked fine and scared at the same time. He wasn't really expecting fire.

Dad: Okay, what's going on?

Me: Dad, Please don't be...

(I sighed.)

Me: The thing that I'm going to tell you is that...

Dad: Why are you running in circles, just get to the point.

(My head started burning, I started sweating.)

Me: It's actually nothing. Never mind.

Dad: What?

Mangi: Baby, come on.

Caught in the Storm

Dad: Baby? Hey, what's going on?

Mangi: Mr. and Mrs. Nkosi. Your daughter is... pregnant with my child.

Dad: Which daughter? Sthoko?

Mangi: It's not her... it's Somi.

Me. Yeah, it's me, Dad.

(Mom's eyes opened wide.)

Dad: What! Mangi, you fooled me? You said you wanted to help my child by being her tutor and you didn't tell me you also wanted to give her babies. I thought you wanted to give her knowledge about Life Sciences...

Mangi: Sir, I...

Dad: I'm not done yet! Instead of giving her knowledge you thought no! This is not enough, I'm impregnating her.

Mom: Honey, calm down.

Dad: You can't tell me to calm down; nobody can tell me to calm down.

Mom: It was a mistake.

Dad: Yes, it was a mistake. Helping him was a mistake, a huge mistake. Not the pregnancy. I thought you were better than the guys in this village, but no! You're actually worse than they are.

Me: Daddy, please. You're being harsh.

Dad: I'm being harsh? Bullshit! Okay, you're pregnant; there's nothing I can do.

Me: Oh, meaning?

Dad: Yes, meaning you should go pack your bags and leave this house, trash!

Caught in the Storm

(There was silence.)

My Dad calling me trash? Tell me it's just a dream. Because no man, no father can call his daughter trash.

Me: Daddy, you kicking me out?
Mom: Honey?
Sthoko: Dad? I know what she did is humiliating, but you can't kick her out.
Dad: Of course I can. Nobody tells me what to do in my own house.

He exited.

(Mangi held my hand and squeezed it just to make me feel less worried. I was crying.)

Me: Happy now, Sthoko? He's kicking me out. I'm pregnant and you're not. Are you glad?
Sthoko: Really?

(She gave me the "are you serious" look.)

Me: Mommy, imagine if it was Sthoko telling Dad she's pregnant. Would he kick her out? Oh wow, we would be celebrating this time and drinking champagne, but just because it's me, it's like I killed someone. Isn't it clear that Dad loves Sthoko? You know what? I'll leave this house. Sthoko, I hope things will be different and perfect without me. Mommy let me go and pack.

Sthoko went to answer her phone outside as it was ringing. Mom was crying.

Me: Mangi, It's fine, you can go.

Caught in the Storm

Mangi: Go? Aren't you going to stay with me?
Me: Are you sure you want to do this, Mangi? I'll be okay.
Mangi: Go pack your clothes.

I went to the bedroom and quickly packed everything.

Mangi: Before I go to the car, Mom, I'll take a good care of your child. I know I don't work yet, but I'll take care of her.
Mom: I'll be so grateful; and I'm sorry for my husband's behaviour.
Mangi: No, it's not your fault. He's just angry and I don't blame him.
Mom: Yeah, I'll be calling you guys.
Me: Mom, help me carry the bags.
Mom: Okay. Will you be going to school?
Me: Of course. So this is how much your husband loves me?
Mom: He'll come back to his senses.
Me: Mom, does he even care about me?
Mom: Come here.

(She hugged me.)

Me: I'll miss you so much, Mommy.
Mom: I'll miss you more, my princess.

We went to the car and Mangi drove.

There's nothing that hurts more than being abandoned by someone you love, someone who means the world to you. Mom couldn't tell her husband what to do. At that point, I felt as though he was not my real Dad. I was hurt; I was heartbroken; I was in pain. What was I going to do? What kind of guy was Mangi? Was he excited about the pregnancy? He didn't impregnate me and run. Was he a South African? Don't tell me you don't understand why I ask this question. Well, people are different in their own way.

Chapter 13

On our way to his house I was just quiet, thinking about everything, how everything is going to change. How my life is going to change. I was going to miss my bedroom. Silly.

Mangi: Baby, you're quiet.
Me: So I'm going to stay with you?
Mangi: Yes, just the three of us in that big house of mine.
Me: The fancy house. Wait? The three of us?
Mangi: Yeah, baby. The three of us.
Me: Who's the third person? We never talked about this.
Mangi: The baby. Aren't you carrying a baby?
Me: (laugh) Seriously now?
Mangi: Ha ha. So the baby's name?
Me: Honey, is this early to give him the name.
Mangi: Oh him, and how sure are you that it's a boy?
Me: I want a boy. I just want to see how you were when you were young.
Mangi: I want her to be a girl.
Me: Baby, that insane, "you want her to be a girl."

(laugh)

Mangi: (laughs) I also want to see how you were when you were young.
Me: Whatever, man.
Mangi: You know we can still be happy. Actually I'm glad you're moving in with me.
Me: Really?

Caught in the Storm

Mangi: Yeah just the two of us, babe. What do you think of that one?
Me: You mean the three of us, ha ha.

We were happy for a while. After a few days things seemed different as I missed my family. It would be three days before I could write Life Sciences. I was so glad we were given enough time to study Life Sciences and we were almost done with exams. Mangi said that he was going to make sure I study every day until I write Life Sciences.

It brought me a good feeling staying with the person I adore, but still I missed home. I mean, home is home. I missed Mom. I missed being around my family, but being with Mangi felt fine too. Mangi loved me, he embraced me, he cherished the moments we shared, he understood me. I was so blessed to have him in my life. In the mornings, he made me feel special by giving me breakfast in bed.

Me: Umm, babe, I'm visiting Thato in few hours.
Mangi: It's okay. I'll be going to the mall after few minutes.

I took a taxi and went straight to Thato's place.

Thato: Friend, I missed you so much.
Me: I missed you too. I've moved in with Mangi.
Thato: You wish girl. Your Dad would never allow that. I mean you're Mom's little doll.
Me: I'm not. Dad kicked me out after when we've told him I'm pregnant and called me a slut.
Thato: What?
Me: I'm not lying.

Caught in the Storm

Thato: And your Mom said?

Me: What was she going to say. Dad is her husband.

Thato: To hell with that. Marriage it's not about one person. It's about two. Your Mom has every right to have a say in a marriage.

Me: That's how marriage is supposed to be.

Thato: Then I don't wanna get married.

Me: But we're happy.

Thato: But still...

Me: I know. I miss my Mom so much.

Thato: It's gonna be fine. Your Dad will come back to his senses, he's just angry.

Me: Yeah, I hope so, friend.

That: So how's you and the baby?

Me: What can I say? We're just fine. You know I can't believe we will be writing Life Sciences soon.

Thato: Say that again.

Me: But I'm ready.

Thato: I know. I'm also ready.

Me: It has always been your favourite subject. I should get going, Mangi's parents are coming in an hour's time and I'm still here.

Thato: Aren't you scared?

Me: I am. I mean I don't even know how they are.

Thato : Let's hope for the best. Bye, see you soon.

It's been two days of staying with my boyfriend and we were happy. He had gone to the mall get me some veggies as he said. I was being treated like a princess and I really adored it a lot. He came back and found me making a cup of tea in his magical silver kitchen.

Mangi: Hey, baby.

Caught in the Storm

(He stood behind me and wrapped his arms around my waist.)

Me: Hun, where are they from?

Mangi: They are from Pretoria, where I grew up.
Me: You don't have siblings?
Mangi: I have a sister who is two years older than I and works as a Biochemist, and also I have a baby sister who's 5 years.
Me: Oh, so tell me a little bit about your Mom and Dad.

(We went sat on the chairs at the table and he was explaining while I was having my coffee)

Mangi: They are rich. My father works as a CEO at the biggest company in the entire Johannesburg, "Ezweni". My Mom is studying in UNISA (University of South Africa) but just doing it to keep herself busy.
Me: Oh, she writes exams online?
Mangi: Yes.

(There was a notification alert.)

Mangi: It's Mom. They're almost here.

Me: Now I'm really nervous, you know.
Mangi: Don't be. It's gonna be fun.
Me: I don't know why, but I'm having this bad feeling about your parents.
Mangi: Oh, you're pregnant.

(He joked.)

Me: That doesn't make me crazy if that's what you're thinking.

Caught in the Storm

Mangi: I'm going to the bathroom. Don't burn yourself with the tea, sweetheart.
Me: Mangi, shut up.

(I hit his arm and he ran to the bathroom)

Me: and you stink (I shouted sarcastically.)

Mangi: (He laughed.) Whatever!

I stayed there for a while. Then suddenly there was a knock.

Me: Baby, there's a knock... Oops he doesn't even hear me, let me go and take it.

(His Mom and Dad were standing before me.)

The mother: I hope we're not lost. Is Mangi staying here?

Me: Yes. You must be his mother.
The mother: I am.
Me: Then, come in.

They didn't like me it seemed. Her words were toxic or I was just imagining things. Mangi's mother was beautiful and his Dad was good-looking too. Mangi looked like his Mom. Don't take it the wrong way; he wasn't gay.

Mangi: Mom and Dad! Arrived earlier than expected.

(He came to the dining room wearing his grey sweatpants.)

His Dad: We know.
His Mom: So, my son, you're still lazy, even now that you just decided to find a domestic worker.

Chapter 14

Oops!
Mangi: A domestic worker? You talking about Somi? Oh no, Mom, She's not the domestic worker. She's my girlfriend.Baby, this is Mom and Dad.

(He smiled and I faked it.)

Me: Oh pleased to...

(I offered her a hand, but she ignored it.)

His Mom: You're what?
His Dad: We've never talked about this!
Mangi: Dad, I know.
His Dad: You always get hurt by dating people you don't even know.
Mangi: I know, now, I've found the piece of my heart. I'm so sure she is the one. Mommy, I've never loved anyone like this.
His Mom: Nonsense, Mangi!
Mangi: What are you saying actually? Are you judging my girlfriend by just looking at her?

(His phone rang. He immediately ran to the bedroom and I wished I could follow him before his parents took out the big forks and started having me as lunch.)

His Mom: What's your name?
Me: Oh me? I'm Somi. Somi Nkosi.
His Mom: What do you want from our son?
Me: Excuse me?
His Mom: Didn't you get it?
His Dad: I'm going to the car. I'll be back.

Caught in the Storm

(He went. I swear this was the worst day of my whole teenage life. What a hard thing to experience.)

Me: I'm not sure of what to answer. Look, Mom, I love your son and I wish you could understand the strong bond between us.
His Mom: I want you to leave him alone. You're too young for him.
Me: I'm just 18, and age is just a number...
His Mom: I don't care, do you hear me?

(Mangi then came to the room where we were.)

Mangi: Mom, did you mean whatever you said?
His Mom: Yes, and you're going to do what I'm asking you to do.

I felt like the world held nothing but sorrow for me. Mangi's face had "anger" written all over it. His hands were on his waist and his breath so heavy as though he was in a running race. It was my first time seeing him this mad.

(Mangi's mother took a phone and made a call.)

His Mom: Look, you can come in now.

(I couldn't understand what was going on.)

Two people came inside. One was a wonderfully dressed girl with a nice body and the other was Mangi's Dad. The girl had a smirk on her face and she glanced at Mangi as though he was her long lost lover. I didn't feel comfortable around her and I could smell bad, hurting news from afar.

Mangi: Mom, Dad, what's going on?

Caught in the Storm

His Dad: Mangi, this is the girl you're going to marry.

Mangi thought: A girl I'm going to marry? Which girl? Somi or Vuyelwa? They want to choose me a wife? What kind of a joke is this? They can't do it in front of my girlfriend, can they? Well, they just did.

Mangi: Dad, you can't let Mom choose a wife for me. This is insane. I have someone I love. This is so crazy. I can't believe you travelled all the way from Pretoria to come and tell me this nonsense. We're not living in the 50s. Even if we were, I'd still say no! Something is seriously wrong with the two of you.

(I stood up and went to the bedroom.)

His Mom: Girls always play with your feelings.
Mangi: How does my dating life concern you?
His Mom: Vuyelwa is the one you grow up knowing.
Mangi: This is so crazy. I'm not marrying Vuyelwa. Do you hear me?
His Mom: That little girl really changed you. She's probably a high school dropout.
Mangi: Mom, my girl is Matriculating and is very intelligent. Not this Vuyelwa girl who failed grade 12 three times. I didn't know your presence was going to be so annoying.
His Dad: We'll be coming again. Think about it, Son.
Mangi: I'm not trying to disrespect you, but Dad, there's nothing to think about!
His Mom: Let's get going. We'll come back.
Vuyelwa: Bye, Mangi.
Mangi: Close the door behind you.

Caught in the Storm

(I heard the door being closed like a prison door and went to the room where they were.)

Mangi: Baby, come here.

(He hugged me.)

Me: Baby, am I losing you?

(Tears filled my cheeks.)

Mangi: Shh no, you're not, Love. Please don't get stressed. I'm not going to change my mind.
Me: Your parents don't love me. They might as well kick me out of their house.
Mangi: You mean my house. They would never do that.

(I've never felt so safe in anybody's arms like Mangi's.)

Me: Look, I need to talk to Mom.
Mangi: You can, but, sweetheart, don't tell her about what's going on. She'll think I'm not taking care of you; she'll think I'm stressing you and...
Me: I won't say anything. Actually, I'll call her this evening. I need to take a nap.
Mangi: Can I come and...
Me: Actually, I prefer being alone.
Mangi: Oh why?
Me: No, Smangaliso.
Mangi: Okay, I'm going to the mall.
Me: For?
Mangi: Some air, I don't understand why you're angry.
Me: Am I angry? Do I look angry, Mangi?

Caught in the Storm

(I was.)

Mangi: I don't know; are you angry, Somi? I'm not going to let our parents nor anyone come between us.

(I kept quiet.)

If only there was something I could do to sweeten this life, believe me, I was going to do it. Only if there was something I could do, I could have done it a long time ago. I wish I knew what the future holds so I could prepare for it.

Chapter 15

Mangi and I woke up very late on this day because he was helping me with Life Sciences and giving me tests just to prepare me for the exam. He surely wanted a bright future for the two of us. He cared about the future and I did too. I've always wanted such a boyfriend. Each and every morning Mangi would wake up first just to whisper "Good morning" in my ear with his accent that made me feel blessed to have him in my life. He did it even this morning.

Our love was like a fairy tale. Our parents didn't like the idea of us being together but that changed nothing at all. I had never thought one day I'd experience such love nor that I'd be in the situation I was. Mangi was not only a blessing, but he was an angel. Mangi beautified my life; he made me jubilant in every situation. He warmed my bones. He would always uplift me whenever I felt down. It was always a series of magical moments with him. It was always mind-blowing and I felt blessed.

I ended up telling him.

Me: You've been nothing but a blessing in my whole lot of life.
Mangi: Well, I came into your life for a purpose.
Me: But Mangi...
Mangi: Yes?
Me: Ah, don't mind at all.
Mangi: Baby, you know that breaks my heart?
Me: Okay I was going to say that my Dad sent me an SMS last night and said that he can forgive me. I can

Caught in the Storm

go back home and stay with them only if you and I break up.

Mangi: What, seriously?

Me: Yes.

Mangi: So what are you saying?

Me: What am I saying? Isn't it obvious?

Mangi: What is it that is not obvious?

Me: Mangi I'm not letting anyone come between us. You can let someone come between us, but I won't.

Mangi: Wow, Somi! I'm also not going to let anyone.

(He kissed my forehead and we were still in bed.)

Me: We don't know, Mangi. You now see you're your parents are following you like bees following a can of a soft, sweet drink.

Mangi: (laughs) Come on.

Me: So you take it as a joke?

Mangi: No, I just find it funny the way you said it. Enough with that, Baby. Look, I'm not choosing anyone over you, not even my Dad.

Me: We will see about that. I'm now hungry.

(I went to the kitchen and opened the fridge.)

Me: Mangi!

(I called him.)

Mangi: I'm coming.

Me: You know we're running out of food. You still have money?

Mangi: I have R1000 left in my wallet.

Me: Where were you getting money all along?

Caught in the Storm

Mangi: My Dad would send me money every month in varsity and he promised to do the same when I came here, weekly, until I get a job.
Me: You think he'll still send the money?
Mangi: He said on Monday, which is tomorrow, but I don't think he'll send it.
Me: Neither do I. So what are we gonna eat the upcoming days?
Mangi: I don't know, but I'm a man. I'll make a plan.

(He said it as though it was the easiest thing to say in the world.)

(Pause)

Me: The choice we made is going to make us suffer, Mangi.
Mangi: Please do not say that, Somi.
Me: The baby needs food. I need food. You, Mangi, need food.
Mangi: The baby, the father and the mother will have food to eat.

(Someone knocked.)

Me: There's your Mom and Dad. You know what? I'm going to do Life Sciences. I'm writing tomorrow.
Mangi: But honey...
Me: Hey, I'm too young to deal with such huge problems like these.
(I went to the bedroom. He went and took it.)

Mangi: Here we go again, Mom and Vuyelwa. What do you want?

Caught in the Storm

His Mom walked into the house as though she owned it, holding Vuyelwa's hand.

His Mom: You know you're such a fool that you don't even think, Mangi.
Mangi: What do you mean now?
His Mom: Tell me, what are you eating since your Dad no longer sends money and since you haven't found a job?
Mangi: Do you care? Do you, Mom?
His Mom: Just stay with Vuyelwa. We'll buy you food.
Mangi: Mommy, I said no. Look I'd rather die by hunger with Somi. I'd rather die with the mother of my child.
His Mom: Why don't you... wait, she's pregnant?
Mangi: Yes, she is and would you just lower your tone because she's writing tomorrow and she's studying right now.
His Mom: You Impregnated her?
Mangi: Yes, and guess what?
His Mom: Oh what?
Mangi: I'm so much excited I'm going to be a father to her child.
Vuyelwa: Ahem, I'm asking water.
Mangi: What are you asking water?

"I, Mangi, was so rude to them and I liked it. What did they want in my house in the first place?" he thought.

His Mom: Haww. She meant that she's asking for water.
Mangi: Okay.
His Mom: Mangi?

Caught in the Storm

Mangi: Mom, do I look like a tap? I mean seriously do I look like a tap?

HisMom: I never believed in witchcraft until today. They bewitched you, my son. Let's leave Vuyelwa.

The storm in my life, getting worse, tossing me, turning me, driving me crazy. I could hear the conversation though I was in the bedroom. Mangi's mother was louder than a freight train. She seemed provocative and I became oblivious to it. The pain I felt was heat, burning me like the flames of hell. Why does it always rain on me? First, it was Kgomotso, then Daddy and now it's Mangi's family. Why am I always forsaken? I felt that I was the slave of life. I was hurt. Life can be so cruel. After one problem comes another, replacing another one or being added to another. Life isn't fair at all.

My brother called me and I was not expecting his call.

Me: Hey, big brother.
Vuyo: Hey, baby sis. How's everything?
Me: Ah, not so bad, you?
Vuyo: Mom told me about everything.
Me: I'm sorry I disappointed you.
Vuyo: No, don't feel like that. It's okay. It's a mistake and there's nothing we can do.
Me: Thanks for understanding, Vuyo. Do you think Dad loves me?
Vuyo: I don't know. I don't think he hates you; he's just furious. Dad doesn't hate you.
Me: Well I hate him. He loves Sthoko.
Vuyo: Yeah, that's a fact. How's you and Smanga?

Caught in the Storm

Me: Not so good. He's being forced to marry another girl from where he comes from. His parents don't want to see me at all.

Vuyo: That's... sad. They are surely up to something.

Me: You think so?

Vuyo: They can't just choose him a wife. That's old.

Me: You know, I'm meeting problems like I'm married.

Vuyo: And you're not married, but growing. So what are you going to do?

Me: I don't know, like, I don't know, brother.

Vuyo: I promise everything will turn out fine.

Me: I hope so.

Vuyo: And good luck in your exam tomorrow.

Me: Thanks.

Vuyo: I love you.

Me: I love you more.

No matter how hard the situation is, how humiliating, how embarrassing, how hurting, or how hopeless, those who love and care about you will always remain and be there for you.

Mangi came straight to the bedroom.

Mangi: They finally left. I was thinking of helping you review Life Sciences as you'll be writing it soon.

Me: Yeah. Good idea.

Chapter 16

Life was now starting to stress me out. Two weeks passed by; we had finished with our exams and it was now December; two weeks without Mom and Dad; two weeks without satisfaction in my heart; two weeks in prison with the love of my life.

Things we do for love are not sweet and soothing, nor are they delightful. The things we do for love are awful. For although love is a very precious feeling that is unbreakable and untouchable, it is also stubborn and blind. I was starting to sleep in the sitting room. Sometimes Mangi would annoy me for no reason. Do hormones work like that?

Mangi: Morning, Somi.

(He walked into the sitting room.)

Me: Morning, Mangi.

Mangi: Look, I'm sorry about my parents' behavior.
Me: It's okay. Will they be coming here again?
Mangi: I don't know. I don't think so. I was thinking that we could go to the mall this afternoon.
Me: Yes, no problem. I hope you made the bed today.
Mangi: Oops! Not yet, but Somi this thing of us not sleeping together Is driving me mad.

(He came closer to my tummy and kissed it.)

Mangi: Let me go and make the bed before my girlfriend strangles me.

I laughed.

Me: You better do it to save your life!

Caught in the Storm

After some few minutes, there was a notification tone from his phone. The phone was on the table.

Me: Baby, there's a message!
Mangi: Open it.

(His voice came from the bedroom.)

Me: You're taking hours to make the bed.

I took his phone and opened the message. It read:

"I really had a great night with you last night. We should do it again. Love, Vuyelwa"

Me: What?

Mangi came to the sitting room.

Mangi: Who is it, my love?

There were tears on my cheeks.

Me: Mangi, you guys made love? Mangi you slept with her really? Mangi why, huh?

Mangi: Baby, What are you talking about?
Me: Don't baby me, Mangi!

(Mangi took his phone from my hand and read the SMS.)

Mangi: Okay, this is actually madness. You need to trust me. This actually wasn't meant for me.
Me: How do I know that? You and I haven't slept with each other in a week.
Mangi: Somi, what? You think I could so such a... You don't trust me?
Me: I don't even know you, Mangi. I don't know you!
Mangi: This is actually madness.

Caught in the Storm

I didn't know what to think. It was actually a very confusing situation. I didn't understand what was going on.

Mangi: I want you to call that number right now.
Me: You know what? There's no need to.
Mangi: Somi, I said call that number!

(He was shouting as if he were my father.)

Me: I don't want to find myself arguing with your girlfriends.
Mangi: What? My girlfriends? Seriously?

Mangi thought: I didn't know someone I love would think I did something as dirty as that. I love Somi and I would never do anything to hurt her. I don't know where she got such poisonous thoughts about me cheating on her. I guess the Kgomotso guy made her lose trust in any boy and he made her worse because she was looking frustrated like a lion that had lost its cub.

I copied the number on my phone and called it.

N: Mrs, Kholoza, hello?

(I hung up.)

Mangi: Voice mail?
Me: It's your Mom.

(Someone should've seen how embarrassed I was.)

Mangi: You know what, I'm going out.
Me: Look, it's not that I don't trust you.
Mangi: Okay?
Me: I don't want to lose you.

Caught in the Storm

Mangi: You, Somi, you are weird. You know what? I'm going out.
Me: But where are you going?

Mangi opened the door and left without telling me where he was going. He banged the door.

Why didn't I trust him after what he has done? Didn't I notice his parents' weirdness? I felt like I've messed up. Mangi's Mom said I had bewitched her son, but who was the witch between us? She planned to break us up. It looks as though it didn't work, but now Mangi is angry with me. I tried to call him and he didn't answer and I didn't blame him. It was now 8 p.m and I was alone in the house. I called Thato.

Thato: Hi, how's everything?
Me: Worse.

(I explained everything that had happened, how Mangi's parents want to choose him a wife and everything else. Mangi had received an SMS earlier on saying "You gave me a good time last night." and it was written that it was from Vuyelwa.)

Thato: No, wait. Don't you think his parents are behind it?

Me: It was his Mom. I got angry with Mangi after seeing the SMS before I knew it was from his Mom.
Thato: But friend, it's like you don't trust him.
Me: I know. I don't trust any guy. After finding that out, he got angry with me. He went out and he's not back yet. He left at 6 p.m. and now it's 8 p.m.
Thato: That's bad. Did you try to call him?
Me: He's not taking my calls.

Caught in the Storm

Thato: He'll come back. Just be patient.
Me: What if he has left me, I'm scared.
Thato: Come on, we are talking about Mangi.

Mangi walked in, finally.

Me: Umm. I have to go. We'll talk.
Thato: I know; it's him.
Me: Exactly. Thanks, friend; bye.

(We hung up.)

Mangi threw himself onto the couch.

Me: You got me worried, Mangi.

(While sitting next to him.)

Me: You weren't taking my calls and I was worried about you. I mean, I know you were angry and still are, but you were not supposed to punish me like that.

Mangi: I'm sorry. I was angry, especially at my mother. Why would she do something like that to her own son?

(He sighed.)

Mangi: I forgive and do not blame you.
Me: Really?
Mangi: Yes. Come here.

(He pulled me and I buried my head on his chest.)

Chapter 17

Days passed by as quick as a flash, yet they were more bitter than a lemon. Holidays felt like nightmares. This was not my best year, especially how it was coming to an end. It felt like a very long, terrifying dream.

In the afternoon, Mangi's Mom came again. She knocked at the door. Mangi went and took it.

Mangi: What?
His Mom: Is this a welcome? Mangi, the girl has bewitched you, hasn't she? Well, why am I even asking? How would you know?

(She was furious.)

Mangi: No, Mama. Vuyelwa is the one who has bewitched you because you were not like this. You were a loving, caring, sweet, mesmerising mother! But now... come in.

(She walked in, looking good as always.)

Mangi: Since when, Mother, have you been choosing a wife for me? Since when do you treat people the way you treat Somi?
His Mom: I want the best for you.
Mangi: It's funny. You don't even know what's best for me, Mama. I'll tell you that Somi is best for me.

(I came into the room where they were talking.)

Me: Baby, I'm having problems with the question paper you gave me this morning... Oh hi, Mom.

Caught in the Storm

(Honestly, I liked her even though she didn't seem to like me.)

His Mom: Hi.
Mangi: I'll come and discuss it with you.

(I was still wearing my pink pajamas my mother had bought and my hair was messy.)

Me: Did you make your Mom tea?
Mangi: She doesn't need it.
Me: Mangi!
His Mom: No, it's okay. I don't want it.
Me: Is everything okay?
His Mom: Mangi, I have to go. Bye.
Mangi: Bye.
Mom: Your Dad was after me, he's coming too.

(She left.)

Me: Are you good?
Mangi: They're stressing me out now.
Me: It'll all pass, I guess.

People: what is love? Love is what was happening between Mangi and me. It's inexplicable.

That evening, Mangi's Dad came and Mangi was not happy at all. I was afraid to say a word to him.

Mangi: Dad, what do you want? I'm getting tired now. I'm tired of you people, busy running on my nerves and you do not get tired!
Dad: You didn't even say "Hi" to your Dad.
Mangi: Hi, Dad. Come in and sit down.

Caught in the Storm

(He sat down and I went to wash dishes in the kitchen.)

His Dad: Mangi, I made sure you stayed in school for 13 years and that wasn't enough so I decided to add four more years so you could go and study Pharmacy. I know it has always been your dream to become a Pharmacist since grade 4. Mangi, I thought that this education wasn't enough so I bought you a house and gave you my own car.
Mangi: And for all that, I'll always be grateful, Dad.
His Dad: Then I ask you a simple, single thing and you refuse to do it.
Mangi: Which is?
His Dad: To marry Vuyelwa.
Mangi: Dad, don't you even care about what makes me happy?
His Dad: Mangi! I'm taking back the car I gave you if you continue refusing.
Mangi: You are not serious, Dad.

(With a worry on his face.)

His Dad: Like Hell I'm not. You know if you continue with this nonsense of staying with this young girl, then you'll realise how serious I am.

Mangi kept quiet. He loved the car with all his heart.

His Dad: Think about it. I'm leaving. Good bye.
Mangi: Close the door behind you.

(He closed it and I came to the sitting room after that.)

Mangi: These people are so mad. I feel that they are walking on my nerves!

Me: They're your parents.

Mangi: I doubt that.

(Suddenly the lights turned off.)

Me: Babe, what's going on?

Mangi: Gosh, the electricity is finished.

Me: Oh no.

Mangi: Babe, can we go shopping tomorrow?

Me: It's okay, but you have only R1000.

Mangi: I'll see what I'll do, hey.

(He scratched his head.)

Me: But, Mangi...

Mangi: Yes, Love?

Me: I think you should just marry Vuyelwa. Look how things have become. Are you enjoying the situation?

Mangi: Then I think I should marry you. Why should I marry her?

Me: Because your parents want you to do that. They're your parents. They've done everything for you.

Mangi: Hey, I don't care! Let them go to Hell.

Me: What if they take this house, I mean, I heard him threatening you about the car.

Mangi: Let them take everything. Yes, let them take it all. I don't care.

Me: Seriously?

Mangi: You know, I think these people are up to something. This is strange.

Caught in the Storm

(Silence.)

Me: So what are you thinking about?
Mangi: Do I even know?
Me: I don't even know what to say. When they take everything, where are we going to sleep?
Mangi: I don't know, I'll come up with something. Baby. I cannot marry someone I don't love. I love you, don't I? Then, I'm going to marry no one but you.

(He held my hand.)

Me: I need to take a nap.
Mangi : You always want to take a nap when we're experiencing something bad.
Me: Something that cannot be solved, yes.
Mangi: What do you mean now?
Me: This! This is...
Mangi: Everything's going to turn out fine, trust me.

(We hugged and then his phone rang.)

Mangi: Ugh! It's Dad.
Me: Aren't going to answer it?
Mangi: Hi.

(He put him on the loudspeaker.)

His Dad: I'll come again on Saturday of next week.
Mangi: Okay.

(He hung up.)

Mangi: This man has changed.
Me: If you need me, I'll be in our bedroom.

Caught in the Storm

It was time for me to see if Mangi was the one for me. I was terrified he was going to leave me. He was stressed. It looked as though he didn't know if he had to leave me or not. He had to choose me over his parents or choose his parents over me. I know that family means everything and that made me feel even worse. It was as though Mangi and I were already married. The problems we were meeting were hard to think about and so difficult to resolve. Relationships are never easy. I tried to figure out why they're like this. I found out that love is involved and when love is involved, love hurts. Again, I tried to figure out why love should hurt, but I came to no conclusion.

I missed Mom so much. She was going to make me feel better. And Dad? I hate him. I don't even want to see him.

Mangi came straight to my bedroom. It wasn't that dark when we lit the candles, but now it was late.

Mangi: Baby, are you fine?
Me: Do I look fine, Mangi? My life is now complicated just because of love?
Mangi: It shows how much we love each other, honey. In spite of all of these sacrifices, Somi, love is the most precious and wonderful thing. It cannot be seen, but can be felt inside the heart. It is full of surprises. It's so very bright as the sun is when it rises.

It creates joy and felicity.

Caught in the Storm

Love is like a brand new jewel that gleams even in the dark.

Love is kind and not easy to find.

It is blind, they say, and sparkling like waters from the river, precious as silver.

You are love, Somi.

Me: No, you are.
Mangi: You are the most wonderful thing; actually you are my Queen. You see, we don't meet people by accident. They come into our lives for a purpose.

The next day we went to Savanna mall for shopping. It was the nearest mall in Fauna Park.

Me: Babe, what's wrong?
Mangi: Why can't I find a job, huh? Now we don't have electricity.
Me: Oh we are no longer going to...
Mangi: No, I don't have sufficient money. I have only R800 for food and you know that you can't eat just anything; you're pregnant.
Me: I know. Meaning we'll have to stay In the dark?

(Question left unanswered.)

We bought food and all the R800 was spent on the food.

Me: You still have petrol?
Mangi: Yes, I think so.

Three weeks passed by and Mangi and I were struggling. Thank goodness we were now finished with exams. It was hard. He had to find a job. He was no longer using his car but taxis. He worked for a week and was paid only R500 and was done with the work. We didn't even know what we were going to do next and Christmas was near.

Chapter 18

The day Mangi's Dad was to come to take or leave his car arrived. I was a bit scared and felt badly for Mangi. I called my brother, Vuyo.

Vuyo: Baby sis.
Me: Hi, you good?
Vuyo: I am. Are you?
Me: No. Mangi and I are in need of money. We currently don't have electricity. We are charging our phones next door. The other day we even slept hungry.
Vuyo: What! Why didn't you tell me? I'll send 5 thousand rand to your account tomorrow. I'm really sorry that it's so little; I'm so broke.
Me: No, that's a lot.
Vuyo: Haaa, really?
Me: I'll will pay you back by the end of this month.
Vuyo: Pay me what?
Me: The money.
Vuyo: Stop bring silly. Good night. I love you guys, you and Thando.
Me: Thando?
Vuyo: The baby inside you.
Me: We love you more.

(Thando? The baby immediately kicked after when I mentioned the name. Thando means love. Yes Thando is a perfect name! Love is the combination of Mangi and me.)

He hung up.

Mangi: That was your brother?

Caught in the Storm

Me: He'll be sending us R5,000 by tomorrow.
Mangi : What! Oh! That's so sweet of him.

(His phone rang.)

Mangi: Hello? Evening, sir... Yes, that's my name, sir... Last month? Oh, yes... seriously? Oh no, I'm so grateful. Okay, bye... You too, sir.

(He put the phone down, jumped and embraced me.)

Me: And?
Mangi: I'm going to a job interview in the nearby hospital tomorrow!
Me: Oh my word! You think you'll get the job?
Mangi: Interviews aren't scary. I've already got the job, Bunny. Oh, I'm so overwhelmed.
Me: I'm so happy for you. Come here.

(We hugged so tight again.)

Mangi: Stress is finally gone.

(We started kissing; you know how it is.)

I received a call from a private number.

Me: Oh, who's this now...
Private number: Hello. Hey, it's your Dad. How are you doing, my daughter?
Me: Dad?
Dad: Yeah. Is everything okay there?
Me: He's asking if everything is okay. What do you want, hey?
Dad: Your Mom and I were thinking of coming that side to talk to you.

Caught in the Storm

Me: Mom can come, but not you! I never wanna see your face again.

Dad: I'm sorry for everything I've done, my baby, okay?

Me: You know what? Good bye.

(I hung up on him.)

Mangi: Your Dad?

Me: Yeah. He feels guilty or something.

Mangi: Oh...

Me: But you know what, I never wanna see him again.

(Knock, knock, knock.)

Me : Baby, there's a knock.

Mangi: ngyeza!

Mangi opened the door.

Mangi: Oh. yeah. Somi come with the car keys.

His Mom & Dad: What? (Simultaneously.)

Mangi: Oh, I'm so sorry. You also want your house?

His Mom: So Mangi, you're just trying to hurt your parents?

Mangi: Actually, you should be excited about getting back your Audi and your fancy house. How am I hurting you?

His Dad: Mangi, we really want that company. I mean just look at ...

Mangi: Excuse me? What company?

His Mom: Vuyelwa's Dad said he'll sell us his company, "The Mthembu Holdings" if we allow you to marry his daughter.

Mangi: What!

Caught in the Storm

His Dad: We could be very rich, Mangi. At least, just ...
Mangi: You're forcing me to marry someone because you want to get rich? All this nonsense just because you want The Mthembu bullshit company? You are not my parents. What about the wealth that you have? Is it not enough? Tell me you guys just adopted me, because seriously, I don't think you could be my parents. You might as well go and tell Vuyelwa's Dad that the plan has failed. Tell him that you even tried to fake an SMS but my girlfriend and I are still doing fine. Now take the keys of the car you bought me. I hate you.

(His Mom was so embarrassed.)

His Mom: Let's leave.

(Looking at Mangi's Dad with an embarrassed look.)

His Dad: Look, you can have the car and the house. We'll be leaving.

(He, too, was embarrassed.)

Mangi was devastated and hurt. I had never seen him so angry before. You would swear I fed him with love portions. I didn't. I was scared and couldn't say a word. I felt guilty somehow and you could tell that I was a little bit down like a chick that had lost the mother hen. Ordinarily, he was a guy filled with tenderness, but this day he surprised me.

Mangi: Are you okay?
Me: Yeah I am. Can I make you something to eat?

Chapter 19

We were now happy. At last we could cuddle in bed again. We had a late night talk. We had fun and the next day in the morning Mangi went to the bank and withdrew the money my brother had sent. At 12 noon, Mangi came back. After a while, I was lying on the couch writing the final chapter of my story "When The Sun Sets" when there was a knock on the door.

Me: Babe!

Mangi, as usual, went and met his parents there.

Mangi: And today you are two. Where's the third one?
His Mom: The third one?
Mangi: Your imaginary daughter-in-law.
His Mom: She's even pregnant.
Mangi: And you wanted me to marry her while she's carrying another man's child?
Dad: We didn't know.
Mangi: Like hell you didn't. Come in.

(They walked in.)

Me: Hello Mom and Dad.
His Mom and his Dad: Hello.

(They spoke simultaneously and smiled.)

Me: You seem to be so happy, especially you, Ma.
His Mom: You know, I've been watching you since I first saw you. You seem to be a good girl.
Mangi: Oh, please. "You xim txhu ve e goo'girl"

(He copied her in a weird, ridiculous way).

Caught in the Storm

Mangi: Baby, let me go to the bathroom.

Me: Okay, love. Well Ma... I don't know about that.

His Mom: I was harsh to you and you never hated me.

Me: I didn't see any reason to do that. Can I make you coffee?

His Mom: Yeah, without milk.

His Dad: I'd prefer one without sugar, please.

They wanted the best for their son, but instead they were about to do the worst. See? We don't simply say people are the real ones simply by seeing them, their shape, smile and any of their deceiving characteristics. Seeing them outside is not seeing them inside.

His Mom: What's your boyfriend doing?

(At last they can call him "my boyfriend". At last they can accept the fact.)

Me: I'm not really sure.

Mangi: I'm coming!

(He walked into the dining room.)

Me: What were you doing?

Mangi: I was looking for what I'm going to wear for the interview tomorrow.

His Mom and Dad: Job interview!

(Again they spoke simultaneously, with excitement.)

Mangi: Playing interview? People!

Me: Baby, really now?

Mangi: These people come here and claim to be nice to us because their "so called daughter-in-law, Vuyelwa" is pregnant.

Caught in the Storm

His Dad: It's not that only. We've just realised that you guys are in love and we can't make decisions for you.

His Mom: Yeah, he's right.

Mangi: Okay, if you say so. Well, it's a job interview, yes.

His Mom: And we're happy for you. Good luck for your job interview.

Mangi: I surely needed it. I couldn't have done it without your support.

Mangi's father's words repeated in his mind. "Mangi, I made sure you stayed in school for 13 years, and that wasn't enough so I decided to add more four years so you could go and study Pharmacy, because it has been your dream since Grade 4 to become a Pharmacist. Mangi, I thought that it wasn't enough so I bought you a house and gave you my own car." My Dad fulfilled my dream. He hasn't been the perfect Dad but he made me the happiest man.

Mangi: Dad, Mom: thanks for everything you've done for me.

His Mom: Come here.

(They hugged and Mangi's Mom's eyes were filled with tears.)

His Dad: Don't thank us, Son. It was a must and our duty.

(He smiled.)

His Dad: Your Mom and I just thought of passing by; we're going to a meeting.

Mangi: Okay, see you another time.

His Dad: Yeah, and thanks for the coffee.
Me: It's a pleasure.
His Dad: Bye.
Me: Baby, you can be harsh, hey.
Mangi: And also I can be sweet. I totally forgive them now.
Me: That's my man.

(I smiled)

(Pause)

Mangi: Meaning you should also forgive your Dad.
Me: What? No!
Mangi: Somi, I'm begging you, okay. Why don't you learn from Vuyo. He forgave his Dad who wasn't there for him for years. Our parents aren't perfectly perfect, but they are still our parents.

Me: Okay! We'll go to his place tomorrow after the interview.
Mangi: Yeah, good idea, ma'am. I love you, okay.
Me: I love you more.

I then received a call from Thato.

Me: Hey.
Thato: Hey. How's everything? How are Mangi's parents?
Me: They're fine. Everything is sorted out. It's just Dad.
Thato: What about him?
Me: He wants forgiveness.
Thato: Are you going to...
Me: Yeah.

Caught in the Storm

(I interrupted)

Me: Actually I've forgiven him already. It's just that he doesn't know.

Thato: (laughs) Why are you always interrupting every time I try to say something?
Me: (laughs) I always know what you want to say. You're my bestie aren't you?
Thato: Yeah, and that's why each and every single thing that I know, you should also know.
Me: Exactly. Is there something I need to know?
Thato: It's your sister.
Me: My sister? Sthoko?
Thato: Yeah. She's dating Kgomotso.
Me: What!
Thato: I'm sorry if this is stressing you out.
Me: No, not at all. I'm just surprised.
Thato: Everyone in the village is surprised.

(Hyperbolically)

Me: Yeah, okay. I'll be visiting them tomorrow.
Thato: Okay, Somi. Bye.

(She hung up.)

That was my friend Thato. She was the definition of love. Her name means love too. I will always be grateful for the love she's given me.

The next morning when Mangi and I woke up, he prepared for his interview. He was in his best suit.

Mangi went and he got the job. We were happy, so we decided to go to my place. I, too, was wearing my best clothes. Mangi and I were looking really nice. I felt alive. We arrived and knocked at the door. My Mom opened.

Mom: Oh, my Doll; I missed you so much!

(She hugged me)

Me: I missed you, Mommy.
Mom: Look at how beautiful you are. Mangi?
Mangi: Hey Mom.
Mom: Thanks for taking care of my baby. Thanks for keeping the promise.
Mangi: It was a must. I love your daughter.

(He glanced at me.)

Mom: Aww... come inside.

(This woman was so excited.)

We went inside. Dad didn't go to work this day. He was the boss at work.

Dad: Welcome. You're both looking nice.

Mangi: Thanks, Mr. Nkosi.
Me: Thanks, Dad. Hi, Sthoko.
Sthoko: Hi. The tummy is now getting bigger. Nice.

(Sarcastically. She was weird.)

Mom: Sthoko?
Me: There's nothing bad in what she said Mom. It is getting bigger, Sthoko.
Sthoko: Well, I have to take a nap, because I'm tired.
Dad: What's wrong with you?
Me: Leave her, Dad.

Caught in the Storm

Dad: We're so glad to have you around. Please forgive me for what happened earlier on. I was just disappointed.

Me: It's okay, Dad.

Mangi: You're forgiven.

Dad: Thanks a lot. How was Life Sciences?

Me: I got total, Dad.

Mom: Wow, seriously?

Me: Yes. Actually, it was easy.

Dad: I'm pleased. Mr Kholoza, do you have a job?

Mangi: Yes.

Dad: Oh, when?

Mangi: Today. I've come from the interview as you see me.

Dad: Wow! Congratulations! I'm so happy for you.

Mom: That's nice.

Mangi: I'll be back. I'm going to the bathroom.

Me: Okay, love.

Dad: You came with your clothes?

Me: My clothes?

Dad: Aren't you staying with us again?

Me: No, I'm happy with Mangi and adapted also.

Mom: Let them stay together, honey.

Dad: And it's okay, hey. Have you seen your beetroots, spinach and cabbages. They've have really grown.

Me: Oh, no.

Mom: Let's go to the garden.

We went to the garden while Mangi was still at the bathroom. When he came out of the bathroom, he met Sthoko in the corridor.

Caught in the Storm

Sthoko: Oops! I thought you were also outside.
Mangi: No, I was in the bathroom.
Sthoko: You know your body is still...
Mangi: Okay. Can I pass?
Sthoko: Come on

(She went closer to him.)

Mangi pushed her.

Mangi: What's wrong with you?
Sthoko: Oh, stop fooling yourself, Mangi. You've always wanted me in varsity.
Mangi: That's what you thought. I was only being nice to you as I realised you were crushing on me.
Sthoko: And the kiss at the restaurant?
Mangi: It was a mistake, okay? Can I please go out now?
Sthoko: It never was a mistake. Come here.
Mangi: Hey, I'm not interested, okay? Now get out of my way.

I went inside the house and found them in the corridor.

Sthoko: So you just called me here to the corridor for nothing.
Me: What!
Mangi: Baby, she's mad. Your sister Is so crazy. I never called her. She just decided to come here and she wanted to kiss me.
Sthoko: You're such a liar, Mangi!
Me: Sthoko, leave us alone, okay?
Sthoko: So you don't trust me?

Caught in the Storm

Me: Yes. You've been acting weird since we arrived here. Is Kgomotso not enough for you?
Dad: What's going on here?

(Sthoko ran to the bedroom)

Me: Your favourite child wanted to kiss my man.
Dad: Sthoko?
Mom: What's wrong with her these days?
Me: She's trying to be herself.
Mangi: Baby, can we just go.
Me: Yeah, Mom, Dad. We're going. Enjoy the remainder of the day. Tomorrow as we'll be getting our matric results, I'll call you and tell you how I did.

We left their house

Chapter 20

In every relationship there'll always be someone who will try to destroy it, no matter how strong the relationship may seem to be. What hurts most Is when the destroyer is someone close to you.

The 5th of January wasn't a sweet day at all, it was terrifying. The grade 12's were getting their results.

Well, it turned out very well. I had passed with 6 distinctions with 90% in Life Sciences. I was very excited. Dad was too.

I'll always be grateful to him for arranging to have Mangi as my tutor. Dad somehow changed my life.

Me: Mangi, I'm so very grateful. I couldn't have passed Life Sciences without your help.
Mangi: I guess I'm the best tutor.
Me: Yeah, you are.

(Pause)

Mangi: What's wrong? What are you thinking about?
Me: You know I'm going to be bored for the whole year.

(I started fiddling with my hair.)

Mangi: I know, hey. Which varsity do you want to go to?
Me: Witwatersrand.
Mangi: What? No. Are you leaving me? How about the University of Limpopo? It's very close. Somi, I can't afford to lose you.

Caught in the Storm

Me: Well, yeah. University of Limpopo is still fine. Can I ask something?

Mangi: Yeah, sure, honey.

Me: Mangi what kind of man are you?

Mangi: What do you mean?

Me: You're phenomenal in your own way. You're kind and your heart is very precious. I want you to know that this love is the best gift I've received in my whole life. I realize we has a lot of challenges and sometimes it felt as though someone was stabbing me by a knife. Mangi, I want to be your wife for the love you're showing me is more than enough.

You say you love me and you don't put a full stop there, but instead you also show me your love by your actions. I know that relationships are not always perfect, but believe me, this love satisfies my soul. If you could see my heart right now, you would see it's full of satisfaction.

Thanks for teaching me all the things I needed to know. Thanks for fighting for our love. Thanks for giving me this love. I love you and I know I have to fully prove it to you as you did. Meeting you was never a mistake. If it were a mistake, then this is my favourite mistake.

I love you so much I'm afraid I don't even know how to show it. I love you and I don't want to lose you.

Mangi: Somi, you've said enough.

Me: No, Mangi. I'm grateful because even my own mother has never showed me the love you're showing. If you leave me, it'll send me straight to death. I swear, if you leave me, I'll lose my breath. I surely was blessed from birth. Please do not ever change in your love for me.

Mangi: Aww, baby, come here.

(We hugged. I cried.)

Mangi: You going to make me cry now.

(I wiped my tears and smiled; then kissed him.)

Mangi: So aren't you going to show your Dad the statement.
Me: You think we should go tomorrow.

Mangi: Yea, So Umama ka Thandolwethu

(So Thandolwethu's mother)

Me: Thandolwethu?
Mangi: Yes, "Our Love". Don't you think it's a perfect name?
Me: It's mesmerising. It best describes the situation. I mean, our love is like a fairytale.
Mangi: Tell me, what kind of man did you want?
Me: I've always wanted a caring man who would make our relationship as wonderful as a bunch of roses, a man who cares about me, a man who's different from all the lions and jackals of this world who would leave you hapless, hopeless and helpless, destroyed, damaged and devastated.
I've always wanted a man who would fill my life with joy and jubilation, making each day of my life a day of jubilee. I've wanted a man who is strong, smart and special. I didn't want a perfect man or a perfect

relationship. I wanted a man who'll be my friend and you're that man.

Mangi: Ah, Somi...

Me: I want to spend the rest of my life with you, not necessarily to be happy for the rest of our lives, but to have you beside me.

Mangi: Of course. Look, Somi, I Love You, okay. I talked to Mom and Dad and told them about your results.

Me: Oh...

Mangi: Yes, and they said we must come celebrate with them. I told them you would agree.

Me: Oh yeah, no problem.

(We hugged.)

Editor

Mr. William Jenkins was born in Ottawa, Canada in 1932. He became a computer programmer and worked in that field for 45 years. Subsequently, he sold residential real estate and then wrote and published a few mystery stories for middle-school children.

After finding publishing using Createspace particularly easy, he began publishing books for others as a free service. There is no charge for the publishing and editing service. See his website
http://williamjenkins.ca.

He is especially interested in publishing stories and poems from students. A few students from South Africa have submitted their writing.

If you are a teacher or student, submit your writing to
williamhenryjenkins@gmail.com.

www.ingramcontent.com/pod-product-compliance
Lightning Source LLC
Chambersburg PA
CBHW071359170626
46811CB00003B/1190